Let Us Be True

A **free** eBook edition is available
with the purchase of this print book.

Let Us Be True | Erna Buffie

COTEAU BOOKS

Edited by Helen Humphreys
Book designed by Tania Craan ·
Cover Photograph by Dorothea Lange. Library of Congress LC-DIG-fsa-8b34383
Typeset by Susan Buck
Printed and bound in Canada at Friesens

Library and Archives Canada Cataloguing in Publication

Buffie, Erna, author
    Let us be true / Erna Buffie.

Issued in print and electronic formats.
ISBN 978-1-55050-635-8 (pbk.).--ISBN 978-1-55050-642-6 (pdf).--
ISBN 978-1-55050-867-3 (epub).--ISBN 978-1-55050-874-1 (mobi)

    I. Title.

PS8603.U523L48 2015   C813'.6   C2015-902952-X
                                      C2015-902953-8

COTEAU
BOOKS
2517 Victoria Avenue
Regina, Saskatchewan
Canada S4P 0T2
www.coteaubooks.com

Available in Canada from:
Publishers Group Canada
2440 Viking Way
Richmond, British Columbia
Canada V6V 1N2

10 9 8 7 6 5 4 3 2 1

Coteau Books gratefully acknowledges the financial support of its publishing program by: the Saskatchewan Arts Board, The Canada Council for the Arts, the Government of Saskatchewan through Creative Saskatchewan, the City of Regina. We further acknowledge the [financial] support of the Government of Canada. Nous reconnaissons l'appui [financier] du gouvernement du Canada.

For Mr. B, who gave me the gift of time…

CHAPTER 1

2000

He can hear the rumble and grind of the carriers, the low-flying thunder of planes. Trees burst into flame, and the night sky rains shells. Khaki ghosts are running into the grim woods at Moyland.

Hansel and Gretel, but this time they're hunting the witch.

The column surges forward at fifty metres a minute. Henry looks to his left. A German flak gun explodes, and Billy Allen is blown out of his carrier. He hits the ground; miraculously, staggers to his feet. His jaw is gone, his neck and shoulders chewed bloody by shrapnel. Henry starts running, but Walter gets there first. He wraps a bundled coat around the gaping wound, and Billy turns, staggering toward the dressing station, down the deep, rutted path left by the armoured column.

Henry steps over dead men, can barely see through the smoke of machine-gun fire and explosions. Up ahead, the cloud clears. A WASP vehicle is stuck in behind a stalled tank, and Joe Walker is standing inside it with a flamethrower in his hands. He swings the weapon back and forth in a half circle, trying to aim it at something, anything, terrified and desperate to kill someone. The trees burn a circle around him. The ground below is a conflagration.

He looks at Henry. *Save me*, his eyes seem to say. *Save me.*

Henry is about to move when it hits – a single bullet slicing through a pressurized tank of jellied gasoline. A flash of white, an explosion loud enough to burst the eardrums, and the Walker boy is gone.

There is nothing Henry can do.

There was never anything he could have done.

She comes to him in the same dream, always. Standing on the platform, her fine, straight hair blown back by the breeze, the hem of her dress rippling just below the knee. She raises her hand as the steam rises up past the compartment window and the train jerks forward. She waves at Henry and shouts, "Bring him back to me!"

"Is there anything you need?"

Henry stares up at the woman standing next to his bed, trying to recollect where he is and where he has just been. She is dressed in white. An angel? Does this mean he's dead?

No. Dead men don't have tubes shoved up their noses and snaking into their arms or a woman in white hovering at the bedside with a needle in her hand. He sees the needle move toward him, feels the pain recede.

"Wake up, Henry. Wake up. They want us over at Ops."

Henry jumps, opens his eyes, feels as if he's just been beaten. His uniform is damp and his back is crammed up against the wheel of a carrier. He's trapped with two hundred other men on the only patch of dry land in sight, surrounded by the flood and the din of amphibious vehicles. Where water meets land, he can see the flat, beached noses of the Buffaloes.

Henry thought he had slogged through water for the last time when they finally pushed the Germans back across the Rhine. By the time that battle was over, he never wanted to see water again. Didn't want to take a bath, couldn't even bear the thought of going for a swim. Month after month, caked in mud, with soaking feet and a wet head and no dry land in sight. It was godawful. The Germans had blown up the Dutch dikes and left them drowning on the polders. They'd even booby-trapped their own dead. But in the end the Water Rats won, and Ike and Monty had given them the winter off.

Now it is happening again.

As soon as they crossed the Rhine, the Germans had started blowing up their own dikes, and once again, Henry found himself plodding, like a half-drowned rat, through three feet of water.

He reaches out, pulls on his boots, happy beyond words to find them dry. He gets up, stretches out his arms and shakes his head.

"Fifteen minutes in twenty-four hours just isn't the hell enough, Walter. Leaves you wishing you hadn't shut your eyes in the first place."

"Well, at least you got fifteen. Baby Face hasn't had

any, and he's already making plans."

"Shit," Henry says, trying to button up his jacket as he zigzags through the klatches of men.

"What I wanna know is how the hell that Colport kid got promoted over you. He must be what, ten?"

"He's a couple a years older than you are, Walter, and he's shit-faced scared just like the rest of us."

"Well, at least if he's shit-scared, he won't do anything too stupid," Walter says.

But Henry isn't listening. He has just spotted Joe Walker fiddling with one of the new portable flamethrowers. Jesus, but he hates those things. Burnt wool and human flesh. Just the memory of it makes him want to gag.

Walter's eyes follow his, and he throws his arms into the air. "Honest to Christ, Henry, every time I see that guy, I wanna rip that thing out of his hands before he hits the wrong button and sends us all to hell. Hard to believe that friend of yours hasn't killed half the company."

"He's no friend of mine, Walter. I just promised Pearl I'd look after him."

Walter shakes his head. "Why that girl wants to marry him instead of you is beyond me. I'd love to meet her. I'd tell her what I think."

Henry grins. "And I'd love to be a fly on the wall when that happened. She'd be up one side of you and down the other as soon as you opened your trap."

"Got a mouth on her, does she?"

Henry nods. "She surely does, Walter."

It was early fall, just two weeks past his eighteenth birthday, and for what seemed to be the first time in ten full years, every field along the road was high with grain. Henry was walking back from town, where he'd just signed up. He was so excited he could barely think straight. Excited and scared witless too, because just a few weeks before, they'd heard the rumors of Dieppe: thousands of Canadians said to be dead or missing, and five of them from right here in town. Henry couldn't imagine it, didn't want to imagine it, because in ten days' time he'd board a train and follow those dead boys across the sea.

He wasn't the only one who would be on that train. Joe Walker and a couple of his friends would be boarding with him. Not that he'd spend any time with that lot. He couldn't stand them, and they couldn't stand him, because Henry loved a good joke, and they liked to drink and carouse. The Bully Boys, he called them, and bullies they were. Sneaky, cowardly and useless to anyone, including themselves.

Henry stopped walking and looked up at the big, wide, open sky. Thank God he'd had the presence of mind to figure out that he actually had a choice about what kind of man he would be.

He was about to start walking again when he glanced to his left, and there she was, striding through the Walkers' wheat field, down toward the creek on the other side, a broad-brimmed straw hat on her head, her blue jean overalls clipped over a fresh white blouse. Henry shouted her name, but she didn't hear him, or maybe she didn't want to hear him, but Henry didn't care. He wasn't going to let her get away this time. So he stepped into the ripe, whiskered wheat and followed her down to the creek.

When he got there, he found her sitting on a rock with her hat in her hand, crying so hard she didn't see or even hear his approach.

"Pearl?" he said.

"Go away, Henry," she said, and turned away from him.

Henry sat down on the rock next to her and decided to take a chance. He reached out, put his arm around her, and to his great surprise and delight, she turned and buried her face in his chest. Then she broke his heart.

"You have to look after him, Henry. You have to keep Joe safe. He can't die, not like my brother."

Colport unfolds the map and spreads it out on the camp table as Henry and Walter lean in. "This is our position," he says, pointing at what looks to be the middle of nowhere. Then he slides his finger slightly to the left. "And this is where I need you to be. It's a hamlet just south of Louisendorf. There's a German battalion hunkered in there, and we need to know what they're up to."

"The whole platoon?" Henry asks.

Colport shakes his head. "Just you, Dennison, Lutz and Allen. Reconnaissance says there's a bombed-out farm right about here. We'll transport you to the road tonight and you can walk in. Should take three, maybe four hours. But watch your step. The Germans are patrolling day and night."

"So what's the terrain? Have the planes been in?"

Colport rubs his eyes. "They dropped a couple of bombs, but the big push is on the bigger towns like Kleve. This is a farm town. Not strategic."

Henry shakes his head. Goddamned air command. No bridges or factories, and it isn't worth bombing, even if there is an entire Jerry battalion sitting on it. A battalion ready to roll out and blow the Rifles and the Reginas to smithereens.

"What time do we go in?"

"Twenty-two hundred, so you better get some sleep."

His stepfather yelled at him, "Get up! Get up, you pathetic little shite. We're going hunting."

"What for?" Henry asked, rubbing his eyes and swinging his thin, thirteen-year-old legs over the side of the bed.

"For whatever we can shoot, stupid. Now get your ass out of bed. It's time to earn your keep."

As if mucking out the hog shed and planting and harvesting what little wheat his crazy, bastard stepfather managed to grow wasn't enough.

Sticks and stones may break my bones, but words can never hurt me.

His mother had sung that old saw to him and his sister Jolene for years, but even at thirteen, Henry knew damn well there were some things that could hurt you worse than sticks and stones and fists. All you had to do was ask his sister.

But he never did ask, because he already knew the answer.

Henry opens his eyes.

How did it get so dark so fast?

He looks to his right and there she is, asleep in the chair beside him. The hospital bed rocks. Henry smiles.

Ted Keeper cuts the engine just as they hit dry land. Henry and the rest of the patrol jump out, give Ted the thumbs up, then wait until he backs the Weasel off the shore and into the water again. A quick wave, and he disappears into the darkness. The men just stand still and listen. Henry waits for two more minutes before he flicks on his flash-light and checks the map.

"Okay, boys," he whispers. "We're this way."

Three hours later, they're hugging the tree line next to a farmer's field. At the end of it, Henry spots a stand of fruit trees. A thin, orange slice of sunrise breaks the horizon and backlights two buildings. Henry can see that the barn is still standing, but half the house has been blown away, leaving the first and second-floor rooms exposed to the world like the split-open side of a dollhouse.

Walter and Bill Lutz move up to walk beside him. "That's the place, eh Henry?" Walter asks.

Henry nods. They're within thirty yards of the house, and he's wondering what the hell they'll find once they get there.

Lutzie stops walking and says what they're all thinking. "Jesus, Henry. If command bombed at night, they were probably all in bed," he says. "I hope to hell we don't find bits of 'em blown all over the yard. I don't think I could take that again."

The words are no sooner out of his mouth than something explodes past Henry's ear, and Lutzie spins back and goes down. Henry wheels around, sees something move near the hay door at the top of the barn: a glint of metal, a whiff of smoke.

Too cocky. They've been too damn cocky.

"Get down!" Walter shouts.

Henry hits the ground, and a bullet slams into the dirt right in front of his head. He crawls under the cover of trees, slides his rifle off his shoulder, draws a bead on the hay door and waits.

"Just shoot it. Shoot the damn thing!"

Henry is lying on the ground, his stepfather next to him. He can feel the man's hot breath deep inside his ear and a rage so white hot that it burns his eyes. He aims, pulls the trigger, and the bull moose goes down. His stepfather leaps to his feet and runs down to the kill. He kneels beside the great dying beast and hoots.

"Beginner's luck, asshole," he shouts.

Henry gets up on his haunches and swallows back the bile that's pushing at the back of his throat. This is his chance. He might not get another. He stands, waits until his stepfather turns to look at him, then cocks the .30-30 and aims the barrel at his head. "Stay the hell away from my sister," he shouts.

Henry stands there long enough to let his stepfather know that he means business. Then he lowers the gun, cracks open the chamber, empties the bullets onto the ground and walks away.

"You did it, Henry," Walter hisses from behind him. "I think you got him."

Henry turns and looks back. Lutzie is lying on the ground, groaning in pain, and Billy Allen lies beside him, trying to staunch the flow of blood from the bullet wound in his shoulder. Henry motions to Walter, and they start moving, crouched low and zigzagging toward the barn. But there's no movement and no firing, so halfway there they stand up and start to walk. Once inside, Henry spots the ladder that leads to the hayloft. He puts a finger to his lips, starts up, and Walter follows close behind. When he gets to the top, he cranes his head up, slow and easy. The body lies a few feet away, its face turned toward him. Henry's own body begins to sway, and he grabs at the floor. He wants to heave, cry out. Instead, he presses his hands into the wood, watches and waits. But he knows by the blood and the size of the wound that the boy is dead, so he climbs up the rest of the way and walks over to stand next to the body. He can feel Walter's hand on his shoulder.

"Ah, Jesus, Henry," he says.

It's a kid, twelve years old if he's a day, and he's wearing a Jerry uniform five sizes too big for him, with a big red hole where his heart should be. Henry stares at the boy and, without a word, picks him up and slings him over his shoulder. The boy is so light. Henry can feel his thin arms slapping against his back, the kid's blood seeping into the khaki fabric of his jacket. The heat of his body is draining out so fast that by the time Henry gets him outside, not even the sun can warm him. So he lays that German boy on the ground, sits himself down and holds the child's hand.

Walter finds a shovel. Before they dig the hole, Henry opens his penknife, cuts a hammered silver button from the boy's jacket and slips it into his own pocket.

"I'll tell you one thing, Walter," he says as he picks up the shovel and slams it into the dirt. "When this war is over, I'll never hurt another living thing."

Henry can hear her shouting at the doctors, but her voice seems so far away. He wishes he could open his eyes, open his mouth, tell her to calm down.

Has he loved her enough? Has he done right by his girls?

But Henry is drifting now, drifting away from the sound and the light, the joy and the pain. He thinks about

Pearl. He's been so lucky. Lucky to be the man that married her, lucky to have lived so long when all those other boys died.

Henry watches as Walter leans his back against a tree and lights a cigarette. The orange glow at its tip pulses, lighting up his friend's face with a soft, strange light. Henry isn't sure which is worse: the terrible noise of the battle or this terrifying silence. They lost half the men in their battalion at Moyland Woods, Joe Walker among them. Henry has a piece of paper on his knee and a pencil in his hand, but he can't think what to write. Maybe he should just let Colport do his job.

We regret to inform you...

Regret. It's something Henry just can't seem to muster for the Walker boy. Not because he was a rival for Pearl's affection but because he was a mean-spirited kid who would have made her life a misery. And Pearl had had enough misery in her life, more losses than any young girl should ever have to bear.

Henry puts the pencil between his knees, pulls out a cigarette and lights it. She won't be an easy woman to love, but he can't think of anything else he would rather do.

CHAPTER 2

2000

She laid them out on the bed. Laid them out like two dead bodies. One was fuchsia, the other the most nauseating shade of turquoise she'd ever seen. She couldn't wait to sell the damn things. Then she'd call up those two ungrateful daughters of hers and tell them what she'd done.

Sold them. That's right. Just put an ad right there in the classifieds and sold them.

Then again, maybe she'd just bloody well give them away. Put them right out there in the front yard and give them to whatever Tom, Dick or Harry wanted them. They didn't fit any more. Size twelve. When was the last time she'd seen a size twelve? The last time one of the girls got married, and it had taken her twelve months of dieting to get there. And for what? Two divorces, one right after the other, and two mother-of-the-bride dresses she'd never wear again.

No one understood commitment these days. No one

had a sense of duty. Spineless jelly bears, the pair of them, with no more sense than a couple of bunnies.

Just like Henry.

Sometimes she wondered if that was why she'd gained all this weight, just to get Henry the hell off of her, night after night, bumping and grinding like a goddamned jackrabbit. But no amount of weight had ever deterred her Henry. *Her Henry.* She'd sometimes wished to God he'd been someone else's Henry, and now he was. Now he was God's Henry, and she was alone with two mother-of-the-bride dresses and two daughters she didn't understand.

What was the point of it all? What was the point?

She had wanted the cheaper casket. She told the girls that. That's what Henry would have wanted, and she agreed. "They're only going to burn the damned thing anyway," she told them.

But oh no, they had to have that great, gaudy oak casket, the size of a Buick that six men could barely lift, let alone carry. What a terrible waste of money that thing had been. And all because of that shiny fat man, the one who spoke so soft she could barely hear him. How he'd led those two girls around by their noses.

"Well, you know," he'd said in that whispery under-taker voice of his. "If you're going to have a service, and you want your loved one there prior to cremation, it's always nice to have a lovely casket. Of course you could always rent one," he added and paused for effect. "But I find that many of my clients tend to be a bit uncomfort-able with that."

Darlene and Carol had reacted as if someone had just let go with a foul odour. Put their father in a used casket? There was no way on God's green earth that was ever going to happen. Not that they'd given a flying fig that

Henry had driven a used car all of his life. They were too far up to their eyeballs in new car payments to notice that.

"We'll take the oak one," they'd sung out like two trained parakeets.

Christ. As if she cared about what the goddamned neighbours or Henry's bowling team thought.

Pearl hoisted herself off the bed, smoothed out the mint green chenille spread and walked down the hallway to the living room. She turned on the TV, and the theme music for *The Price Is Right* boomed out of the console. She stared at Bob Barker.

"Jesus," she said to herself. "Is that man ever going to die?"

The day after the church service, after Henry had been cremated, they'd all gone to the cemetery for the burial. They'd been standing on the snow-blown prairie for what seemed like forever, while that silly young minister droned on, when the shiny fat man from the funeral home picked up Henry's urn and started waddling toward the hole in the ground they'd dug for it. As soon as he started to move, Pearl felt her hands twitch and a strange kind of panic take hold of her brain. Her feet moved forward, her hands reached out in front of her, and all she could think about was getting Henry away from that sweaty little man.

"Give him to me," she said, her voice booming across the cemetery like a great, godly clap of thunder. On her charge to intercept him, she saw her daughter Carol roll her eyes heavenward as if to say, "Oh God. Take her. Please, take her."

Oh, get over yourself. Just get over yourself. He'll take

me soon enough, Pearl thought as she swiped the $395 urn out of the penguin's hands. Holding it against her chest, she carried it to the grave, bent down and put Henry's last remains in the hole. Then she did what she'd seen dozens of other women do in the movies and on TV. She bent down, picked up a handful of dirt and stared at it. It was just a handful of dirt, but it felt as if it might burn a hole in the palm of her gloved hand. So she tossed it into the tiny grave like a hot coal, cleared her throat and stood up to face the assembled crowd.

"It's time for tea," she said, pointing at the big, overblown, black and shiny $150 a day limousine. "Let's get this show on the road."

Pearl stared out the living room window. So what if she had been a bit loud? At her age, she didn't have time to stand on ceremony. She looked down at the double-decker end table and picked up Carol's grade twelve photograph. Carol had always been such a pretty little thing, so sweet and thoughtful, at least until she turned sixteen and that boy came along. Now Carol was almost fifty, and all she seemed to care about was that bloody house of hers. Two days before Henry's burial, she'd begged to have the funeral tea at her place.

"It's bigger, Mom," she said, when what she really wanted to say was that it was nicer to look at.

Carol lived in one of those new subdivisions, with a stone kitchen counter, an oven in the wall and a living room big enough to hold a wedding reception. And all she ever did was buy things for it. New things. Used things. Useless things. Like that second toilet you couldn't pee in. Pearl had turned the tap on it one night after dinner and got a jet stream of water in the face for her trouble. Carol's sons had almost fallen off their black, lacquered dining room chairs when she told them what she'd done.

Imagine. Grown men laughing at their grandmother. Pearl had just picked up her purse and headed for the door.

"Oh for goodness' sake, Mother, don't be silly," Carol said. "Come back and have your dessert."

On the way home, Henry had tried to reason with her.

"You have to admit, Pearl," he said. "It was pretty funny."

Well, it hadn't been funny to her. It was humiliating not knowing what that second toilet was for, and those two grandsons of hers should have known better. No, she was never going back to Carol's house. Why the hell should she? Her daughters rarely came to her house. They were embarrassed by it. Even though it was always dusted, always spic and span and shiny clean, both of them thought it was a dump. Oh, they never came right out and said it, but Pearl could see them cringe when they walked in the door. Like the day Darlene brought that girlfriend of hers to the house for the first time. Now what the hell was her name – Athea? Altia? No, that wasn't it. There was an "n" in there some-where. That's right, Athena. That's what her name was, and a godawful, silly name it was too.

Not that it mattered. Pearl liked Athena. Liked her bet-ter than most of the idiot men her daughters had dragged into the house. The day they met, Darlene had arrived in a huff, ready to do battle, as if it were Pearl's inevitable intention to embarrass them both or reject the girl. But Athena had just reached out and hugged Pearl as if she were her own mother, then plopped herself down on the couch, looked at the sausage rolls on the coffee table and blurted out a story about one of her spa clients that had left Pearl in stitches. In this respect, Athena was a lot like Henry, and Pearl had hoped against hope that some of her cheerful nature might rub off on Darlene, because truth be told, her daughter could use a bit of lightening up. But Athena's lightheartedness had not rubbed off on Darlene any more than Henry's constant clowning around had made Pearl the life of the party. Some people were just born serious, and if anyone fit the "deadly serious" bill, it was Darlene. Always on about this or that, always making an issue where there was no issue to be had or wanted.

Like the day she and Athena had walked in the door for the funeral tea. Even though Pearl had made it perfectly clear that she didn't give two hoots what they did in that bedroom of theirs, Darlene just couldn't leave it alone, couldn't help throwing it in her mother's face. Putting her arm around Athena, right there in front of everyone, and telling them all she was a lesbian. As if nobody over the age of seventy knew what a goddamned lesbian was. Like they all hadn't figured it out when the two of them walked in holding hands. In the midst of it all, she caught a glimpse of Athena's face and knew that she wasn't any happier with Darlene's public announcement than Pearl was, and for that alone she would have liked the girl. Because she just seemed to know that some things were best kept private.

Pearl shook her head. For a woman with a PhD, Darlene could certainly be a silly ass sometimes, and as far as she was concerned, the blame for that lay squarely with Henry's side of the family. She just hoped to God that Darlene was sensible enough to know how lucky she was.

Pearl set Carol's photograph down on the end table and stared out the window at the dilapidated house across the street. Her daughters' lives were so different from her own. She'd been the one to see to that. Not that they appreciated her efforts. Not that it had made one goddamned bit of difference. All you had to do was look at Carol's life to see that. Lording it around in that house of hers, with her two spoiled sons and that bland, blond-haired milquetoast she'd married. About as much personality as a dishrag, that one. Not a bit like Henry. At least Henry had known how to laugh.

Well, to hell with the lot of them. This was her house, and she could do as she damn well pleased with it. She turned to scan the living room then stopped. It was so quiet in here these days. Not at all like it was when Henry was alive. How many times had she prayed for a day just like this – a day with a little peace and quiet, a day with no Henry? Now that day had finally arrived, and she didn't know what to do with herself. She needed to get busy. She needed to keep moving. Maybe she'd just cancel that classified ad and have a big garage sale instead.

Pearl looked up at the wall above the couch. That moose head of Henry's would be the first thing to go, and she still hadn't emptied out his closet and drawers, so all of his clothing could go as well. Then there was all that crap the girls had left behind when they got married. The things they didn't want her to throw out. Well, to hell with that. She'd been storing that junk for more than twenty years, and it was long past time to get rid of it. Maybe she'd even sell that ridiculous food processor thingy Carol had given her last Christmas. What a silly piece of hardware that thing was. Just took up good counter space.

She'd have to make sure Carol came to the garage sale. Maybe she'd take the hint.

Then there were all those books Darlene kept giving

her. Books to improve the mind. "Novels," Darlene called them. *Novels, my ass.* She'd take a good Harlequin romance any day, or one of those Frank Yerby historicals. And that James Michener, now there was a man who could write.

Pearl glanced around the room again, her eyes coming to rest on the pine couch and matching rocker with its threadbare yellow, brown and white tartan upholstery. She looked at the Arborite coffee table with the nick in the corner and the pole lamp with its egg-shaped shades, with the squiggly lines and brass fittings.

Christ. Maybe she'd sell the whole lot. Just get rid of it all. Maybe she'd sell the house and get a nice piece of land outside the city where the farm used to be. Pearl stared up at the faded yellow wallpaper Henry had hung in the living room more than twenty years before and wondered if there was a heaven and if Henry was up there with the rest of them. In the months since he died, she'd sometimes felt as if he were standing right behind her, watching her like he used to do. Well, if he were lurking around now, he'd be none too pleased with what she was about to do. But Henry never had liked change, whereas she'd been forced to get used to it.

"No time like the present" was her motto. You just had to bear down and get on with it. Pearl straightened her back, walked into the kitchen and started to get organized.

She called her two friends, Izzie and Jean, and they arrived the next day to give her a hand. They argued with her, of course. Tried to talk her out of it.

"When my Charlie died, my mother told me, 'Don't do a thing.' Don't sell anything and don't move house no matter what anyone tells you," Jean said. "Give yourself at least a year."

"Jesus Christ, Jean, you were forty-two when Charlie died. I'm seventy-four. I may not last the year. Now, empty out that cupboard," Pearl said.

Izzie wrapped an arm around Pearl's shoulder. "Maybe I should call Darlene and Carol. Get them to give us a hand."

"No. They'll just get in the way," Pearl said as she turned and stomped off down the hallway. "I'll be in the bedroom. I got a few things in there I need to sort out."

Hidden in a cubbyhole above the top shelf in the bedroom closet, she found the box she was looking for, the one with the photographs she'd always meant to throw away. Holding the box in one hand, she reached out for the doorframe with the other and stepped down the three-stair ladder she'd dragged in from the kitchen.

Not bad for seventy-four.

Pearl put the shoebox on the bed, sat down and stared at it, debating whether or not she should open it. In the end, she decided it wouldn't make much difference either way, so she lifted the lid, reached in and picked up the top photograph, its edges the dirty yellow-grey that sets in with age. It was a picture of the old farmhouse. Her mother sat in a rocking chair on the front porch, her father stood beside her, and the three kids, Matthew, Winnie and Pearl, sat on the top step.

Pearl closed her eyes. How she had loved that house. Every second morning the rooms were filled with the smell of blooming yeast and butter. In the kitchen, her mother sat playing solitaire, waiting for the first batch to bake, smoking one of her hand-rolled Black Cat cigarettes. And summer, winter or fall, the kitchen window, fogged up by the scalding-hot dishwater her mother poured into the sink.

Wash, drain and dry. Wash, drain and dry: morning, noon and night.

And just outside the kitchen, in the dining room that wasn't a dining room, were the bags of remnants, her mother's treadle sewing machine and the endless pile of rag rugs she ran off, day after day. Red and black and purple; yellow, navy and brown; grey and burgundy: a steady stream of fabric and colours, all braided together with no rhyme or reason into a swirling oval pattern of her father's old top coat, her mother's worn-out house dresses and the children's outgrown overalls.

Where had all those rag rugs gone? Her mother hadn't sold any of them. Pearl's aunt and uncle must have thrown them out or given them away after the funeral.

Jean popped her head through the bedroom door. "Pearl?" she said. "Are you in here? Tea's on."

Pearl opened her eyes. "I'm over here, Jean."

Jean tiptoed through the piles of Henry's clothing stacked on the bedroom floor and looked over Pearl's shoulder at the photograph. "Oh my," she said. "There's the old farmhouse. And there's your mother. She was such a lovely person."

Pearl stared at the photograph and frowned. "Yes, she was," she said, tossing the photograph back into the box. "But she married a bad man."

"Such a tragedy," Jean said, shaking her head. "I always thought you were so lucky to have Henry. He was such a kind person."

Pearl turned and looked up at Jean. She opened her mouth and closed it. Opened and closed it again. Then she felt something she hadn't felt since she didn't know when:

a soreness in the back of her head, a tightening in the tendons of her throat. When she spoke again, her voice was as quiet as Jean's, as quiet as it had been in quite some time.

"I've got to finish up in here. Just keep the tea warm. I'll be there in a few minutes."

When Jean left the room, Pearl put the lid on the box, pushed it away and stared at a pile of Henry's old flannel shirts. She had been in love with Joe Walker, but fate had given her Henry.

"Horse shoes up the bum," he said, grinning like a baboon on that sunny day in 1947 when she ran into him on the main street of town. "Got shot in the leg, got shrapnel in the arm, but I made it."

He made it. But Joe Walker did not.

Pearl had been fourteen when she set her sights on Joe Walker. Joe was seventeen. He had thick, black hair, big arms, and he was wild – wild as a barn cat. Charming one minute, his mouth as mean and nasty as a prairie dust storm the next. How many times had he left her, face red and stinging, eyes tearing up, lungs gasping for air? But when he was good, Joe made up for all of that, and Pearl had loved him with the kind of blind, crazed, full-tilt passion only a fourteen-year-old could muster.

But Joe had died in the war, and she had married Henry.

Henry Calder.

Couldn't be balder.

When he was a kid, no one ever wanted to play with Henry, because he stank to high heavens of pig shit. Every morning at four a.m., his stepfather dragged him out of bed to muck out the hog shed, and he never had enough time to clean up properly before he left for school. So Henry had become one of the untouchables. But instead of turning him into a nasty boy, it made him a joker.

"Hey, girls," he'd call out to them at recess. "I got a bottle of perfume just for you." Then he'd hold up a quart sealer jar, half-filled with watery pig crap, and all the girls would shriek and gag in disgust while Henry laughed like a loon. Laughed so hard, he almost fell over.

He was like that until the day he died. Henry loved a practical joke, and he loved it when Pearl got in a huff and yelled at him when he pulled one over on her. Like the morning he'd put a whoopee-cushion on her chair. She'd been so mad at him that she'd slugged him with the cushion, leaving a big red welt on his arm.

"Oh, now. Pearlie," he said, "look what you've done. Now you've got to kiss it better."

He started toward her, but she took off at a run, and he chased after her, making monster noises and grabbing at her shirt. She tried to stay mad, but she started to laugh, and she laughed so hard, she thought she'd pee her pants. So she ran for the bathroom, locked herself in and refused to come out. But Henry wouldn't stop laughing and pounding on the door, so Pearl got mad all over again and yelled at him through the keyhole.

"Go away, Henry. I won't kiss your goddamned arm. I don't love you. I never have, and I never will."

Pearl had spent quite a bit of their married life shouting nasty things at Henry, but it hadn't made one whit of difference. He never left, never raised his voice or a hand to her. He was like an adoring dog that got in under your feet and wouldn't leave you alone, no matter how many times you pushed it away.

And that was why the girls had loved their father and why they didn't like her. He was for fun and play. She was for bitching and scolding. And there was no changing that.

Her daughters didn't need her, and she certainly didn't need all this junk in her house. What she really needed was a cup of tea.

Pearl stared at the box of photographs on the bed and decided that there was no great rush. She'd throw them out tomorrow, after the sale was done. She got up and accidentally kicked over a pile of Henry's sweaters, but when she bent over to straighten them, she found she couldn't bear the thought of touching them again, so she stepped over the mess and headed for the kitchen.

The day of the garage sale, Izzie and Jean arrived at seven a.m., and the three of them lugged and hauled and carried until everything was outside.

"I don't know why you want all this stuff in the front yard," Izzie said. "If I was your neighbour I'd be pretty put out."

Pearl smiled. "That's the whole point," she said.

Pearl couldn't stand her neighbours. Not one on either side. The old coot on the right was forever running around with that bloody leaf blower of his, leaving great huge wads of paper and grass clippings under her hedge. And that silly young woman who lived on the other side was just like Carol. Always telling Pearl how cute her house was and how wonderful it would look with a fresh coat of paint. Well, if she wanted Pearl's house painted, she could pay for it. Pearl had no intention of flushing Henry's pension money down the toilet. There was little enough as it was.

By seven thirty, everything but one box was out, and Pearl chased her two friends into the kitchen to make another pot of coffee. Now, she carried the last cardboard box from the basement storage room out onto the porch. Setting it down, she sank into the white and yellow lawn chair. Its metal frame dug into her thighs, and the three-inch plastic straps of its basket weave seat strained under the wide weight of her bottom.

Pearl surveyed the contents of her house spread out across the lawn. She'd left the big-ticket items – the living room couch and the girls' old twin beds – in the house. She had kept only the essentials: the good flatware and china, the bedroom set and the dining room suite, and the best of her pots and pans. From now on she would only use the good stuff. No more waiting for company. No more saving it for the grandkids. She wouldn't be like her aunt Clara, dying with all of her "for good" things locked up in a cedar chest or gathering dust on the top shelf of a kitchen cupboard. These things were hers. She had picked them, and now she was going to use them every single day for the rest of her life.

Pearl yanked on the crisscrossed flaps of the last cardboard box until it popped open. She peered inside. The smell of mothballs and memory floated up to greet her as she reached out to touch the rough, khaki-coloured wool and tarnished brass buttons of Henry's old army uniform. When had he packed this away? It must have been fifty years ago.

Lifting the uniform out, she set it down beside the box. Under it, she found Henry's old marching boots, the tops folded down at the ankle, his kit bag, a canteen and a box of beribboned medals with a hammered silver button nestled inside. One by one, she picked up these small, forgotten fragments of Henry's life and gently set them on the porch. Then she turned back to the box, pulled out a layer of yellowed tissue paper and stared at what was hidden inside. She pushed herself back in her chair and gripped the plastic armrests so hard she heard one of them crack.

He had no business keeping these things when she had told him to throw them out.

"I've got my own life, now," she'd said. "It's time to get rid of the past."

But instead of throwing her past into the garbage, Henry had put it in a cardboard box and hidden it in the basement. Her family, risen from the dead, resurrected in the things they had loved: a book of poems, a packet of letters, a pocket watch and a pair of silver shears. And beneath these small mementoes, the pink and blue rag rug, the one her mother had made for her the summer she turned twelve. The summer her brother, Matthew, had gone to war, and she and her sister, Winnie, had gone to live with their aunt and uncle. The summer Pearl's father had killed her mother then hanged himself in the barn.

Pearl closed her eyes. They were all gone now, her brother, her sister and her parents. They had all left her, just as Henry had left her, just as her daughters had left her now. They'd left her alone to fend for herself, and that's what she had done, because that was what she had always done.

Pearl laid the rug across her lap, straightened her back and stared at her life spread out across the lawn. The scimitar blade of the food processor glinted in the sun. Next to it, on the black tin tops of the TV tables, were the stacks of books and boxes of Yardley soap, rose and lavender and lilac – drugstore soap she never used but which Henry kept stuffing into her Christmas stocking year after year. And beside them, the last of the Tony the Tiger glasses he'd collected with every refill at the Esso station, the one where he'd worked for more than thirty-five years.

Pearl stood up, reached for the porch railing, and the rug slipped from her lap. She bent down to pick it up, and as she did, the blood rushed into her ears and up through her head and the world went into a spin. But Pearl kept on moving, step by step, down the vast expanse of porch stairs and into the yard. And as she walked, she touched things. The miniature china spaniels Carol had given to her as a birthday gift, Darlene's tin dollhouse with its brightly coloured plastic furniture, and next to it, the Chinese Checker game Henry and the girls had played every night one winter, played until the girls were good enough to beat him. And in an old Eaton's box, the faded pastel-coloured baby clothes she'd knit for Carol and Darlene and the child who hadn't survived.

"Oh Lord," she said as she reached out for a TV table to steady herself. "What have I done?"

She turned toward the house. "Henry," she called out, and when no answer came, she called again, louder this time.

"Henry!" she shouted, and as she did, the TV table gave out from under her, and the ground came up to meet her.

CHAPTER 3

1944

Winnie hated dresses. Even as a little girl she had hated
them, hated having to wear skirts to school and absolutely
dreaded putting on her "Sunday-go-to-church clothes."
She didn't like hats either: Easter bonnets with ribbons
and silly cloth posies, Sunday school broad-brims that
blew off in a strong prairie wind, even when you nailed
them to your head with a lethal-looking hat pin. Winnie
preferred a woolen toque with a bit of stretch that hugged
her head, a pair of denim overalls and a good, strong, flat
pair of shoes. Feminine things just didn't appeal to her,
and she never knew why until she started her after-school
job at the Nighthawk Diner and met the lovely Jolene.

Jolene Calder was twenty-one and had blond wavy hair
and a small wavy body. The kind of woman who could
make anything look good, even their starched pink waitress uniforms, with the black piping and lacy flowered
hankie in the breast pocket. While Winnie always came
out looking like a well-chewed piece of pink bubble gum,

no matter how many times she starched and pressed her uniform or how artfully she arranged her handkerchief.

"Some women just look better in pants," Jolene said when Winnie expressed her loathing of all things involving a skirt. "There's not a lot you can do about it. Just thank your lucky stars you look good in something." Jolene grinned and flung her thumb over her shoulder. "Look at poor old Elsie over there. Wouldn't matter what she threw on, she'd still look like a goat."

Winnie had clapped her hand over her mouth to keep from laughing, because Elsie Hermann had a black moustache on her upper lip and three chin hairs so long she could almost braid them. Thank God Winnie didn't have that problem. Her face might be a bit round and a little too flat, but she had perfectly smooth olive-brown skin like her mother and thick black hair that was shiny and straight. So straight that despite her aunt Clara's best efforts, it never did take a perm. No matter how many hours Winnie sat enveloped in a nauseating cloud of ammonia fumes, with fat strands wrapped so tight on the bone-shaped curlers that her eyes were squints and her scalp screamed for release, her hair always unrolled just as it had gone in – flat as a board.

And that was fine by Winnie, because she liked her hair long and crisscrossed into a thick plait that lay flat down the length of her spine. It kept it out of her face, and it was the one concession she could make to being a woman, when in truth she would much rather have been a man. She would have preferred to walk and talk like a man, to wear men's clothing and do a man's job, but no one would let her, so she kept those thoughts to herself. There was no sense upsetting people, and besides, telling them wouldn't have made any difference. Whenever she had brought it up in the past, people had treated her like she was nuts.

"I want you to call me Will," she said to her mother on a summer day when she was six years old. "My real name is Will, and that's what I want you to call me."

"Wherever did you get a notion like that?" her mother asked, looking up from the solitaire game she was playing at the kitchen table. "Winifred is such a pretty name, and I chose it especially for you. Why don't you like it?"

Winnie didn't want to hurt her mother's feelings, but she wasn't old enough not to tell the truth. "It's a nice name, Mama, but I'm not really Winnie. I'm Will."

"Then you can be Will today, but you'll go back to being Winnie tomorrow. Now off you go. Go outside and play."

Winnie had lingered at the kitchen table, watching as her mother turned up a king and moved her queen, jack, ten to sit on top of it.

"Say 'Will,' Mama," she said quietly. "Say, 'Go outside and play, Will.'"

Her mother squinted at her through the smoke of her Black Cat cigarette with such an odd look on her face that Winnie decided to do as she'd been told. She ran out of the room and out the door, past the barn and down to the creek, where she sat down on a rock.

"I'm Will," she said to the slow-running water.

In the end, she decided that it didn't really matter if no one else knew that she was Will. It only mattered that she did. But when she turned seventeen and met Jolene, the fact that she was Will suddenly mattered again. It mattered very much.

She was walking to school with her sister, Pearl, when she finally broached the subject. "Do you ever think about going back to the farm?" she asked.

"Never," Pearl said. "I'll never go near that goddamned place again. Not after what he did. I wouldn't touch it. Not if you paid me."

"But it's ours. Shouldn't we do something with it?"

"We don't have to do anything with it. We're girls. You're a girl. If Mattie had lived he would have run the farm, but he's dead now, so that's that."

"But I want it. I want to run the farm. I know I can do it."

"Don't be ridiculous, Winnie. You can't handle something like that on your own, for Christ's sake. Marry a farmer who's got his own place, and leave that one to Eddie. He's going to get it anyway."

Their cousin Eddie was a little shit, and even if he hadn't been a little shit, Winnie still wouldn't have wanted him to have the farm. She was the one who needed it. She had to have it.

She set her chin. "It doesn't belong to Eddie. Dad left it to Mattie, just like his dad left it to him."

Pearl threw up her hands. "So what! It needs a man to run it, and Eddie's in aggie school studying to be a farmer. And besides, we don't need that place. I'm going to marry Joe when he gets back, and you'll find someone to take care of you. And besides, Aunt Clara wouldn't let you have the farm even if you begged. Her precious little Eddie is going to get it. And let him have at it, I say."

Winnie stopped walking and stared at her sister's back. It was all well and good for Pearl to say she didn't want the farm. It didn't really matter to her. Pearl was the right kind of girl. She'd do fine without it.

Pearl stopped walking and turned around. "Now what?"

"I want it, Pearl. I want the farm."

Pearl stamped her foot on the ground, and a cloud of yellow dust puffed up around her ankle socks and blew off into the air. "Jesus H. Christ, Winnie. Why can't you just be like everybody else for once in your goddamned life? Why can't you just want what you're supposed to want?"

Winnie held her ground, and Pearl relented. "Fine. Go ahead and ask, but I'm telling you right now it won't do any good." Without another word, she turned down the path that led to school, and Winnie followed.

Jolene had a coffee pot in one hand and two plates of ham steak with mashed potatoes and peas balanced in her right. "You should wear the grey wool pants. They've got those nice pleats in the front, and they suit you."

"I don't know," Winnie said as she poured sugar into a glass dispenser. "I don't think I'll go. I don't really like to dance."

"You'll never find a boyfriend that way," Jolene said with a wink as she swooped off to deliver her plates to the two good-looking pilots sitting at table number four. They were air force trainees, two of the hundreds of boys who drove in from the airstrip just outside of town, ostensibly to eat at the Nighthawk Diner but mainly to look at the lovely Jolene before being sent off to die in the skies over Europe. They grinned at each other as she poured their coffee. Then one of them said something, and Jolene's face turned red. She turned on her heel and walked away from their table, past the counter, all of the swoop and bounce gone from her step.

"Men are such pigs," she said under her breath and slammed the coffee pot back onto the burner. Her expression was hurt and confused when she turned to Winnie. "Tell me the truth. Is my uniform too tight?"

Winnie looked at the pink skirt of Jolene's uniform stretched taut around her hips, the narrow angle of her small waist, the way her right breast strained against the fabric beneath her lace hankie. She wanted to go over and slug that fly-boy for whatever he had said to upset her.

"You look great. You always look great."

Jolene threw up her hands. "Then why do they say things like that? Why can't they just be nice and polite and leave me alone?"

Winnie shrugged. "Because they're men, I guess."

"Well, I'll never marry a man like that. I want someone who respects me. Someone who thinks I'm the cat's ass," Jolene said, lifting her chin and crossing her arms against her chest.

Winnie stared at the saltbox. "I don't think I'll ever get married. I want to run my own farm."

Jolene laughed. "Then you'd better change your mind about getting a husband. Or come to the dance and find yourself a big, strong hired hand."

Winnie frowned and moved on to filling the salt shakers. She could feel Jolene's eyes on her, heard the rustle of her skirt as she began to move, the breezy sound her nylons made as they rubbed against her thighs. She could feel the heat of Jolene's body as she walked up to stand beside her, the warmth of her hand as she reached over to rest it on Winnie's arm.

"Jesus," she said. "You're serious, aren't you?"

Winnie pulled her arm away, shoved the small, tin funnel into the neck of another saltshaker and nodded.

"You are one strange girl, Winnie," Jolene said as she moved off to take an order from the farmer at table five.

"What?" Her aunt Clara looked up from the sliced leather she passed off as roast beef every Sunday and stared at Winnie. "What did you say?"

"I said I'd like to go out to the farm and look it over. I think I'd like to run it when I finish school."

Clara snorted. "Eat your dinner, Winifred, and stop talking such nonsense."

Winnie opened her mouth to protest, but as usual, Pearl beat her to it. "It's not nonsense," she said, placing the fisted butt ends of her fork and knife onto the table. "That farm belongs to us. It belongs to Winnie and me. I don't want it, but she does, so it should go to her."

Clara looked at her husband, Edward. "Did you hear that, Father?"

"I heard it, Mother," Edward grunted as he sawed on a grey slab of meat. Winnie watched as he shoved an enormous chunk into his mouth, started to chew, then aimed his knife first at Pearl, then at her. "Now let's get this straight. That land belongs to your aunt Clara and I. It's payment for the two of us taking you in. Neither one of us wanted you, but we did what was right. If it had been up to me, you would have been shipped off to live with your mother's family, but Clara wouldn't have it. So we fed and clothed you and sent you to school just like you were our own. But when Matthew died, that land reverted back to your father's family, and that means your aunt Clara and me. And by God," he said, slamming his knife hand onto the table, "we'll give it to whoever we damn well please. And I don't want to hear another word about it."

Winnie stared at the expression of smug triumph pasted across her aunt's stiff little features and knew that this was a battle that had long been lost. But Pearl refused to give up. She got to her feet and threw her napkin on the table.

"You've got no right. You've got no goddamned right."

"Well then, missy, you can just pack up your bags and move on if you don't like it. I'd be quite happy to see the back end of you walk right out that door," Edward said, flicking his knife in the air. "You're an embarrassment to us all. Chasing that Walker boy around before he left. Throwing yourself at him. You're nothing but a foul-mouthed little slut. And that sister of yours," he said, pointing his knife at Winnie. "God in heaven knows what the hell she is. Half the time I can't tell if she's a girl or a boy."

Pearl lunged across the table, arms outstretched as if she was about to throttle him. Winnie got to her feet and grabbed her sister's shoulders.

"I'll kill him," Pearl said, her hands bunching into fists. "I swear to God, I'll kill the son of a bitch."

"Just leave it, Pearl," Winnie said as she pulled her sister away from the table and out through the dining room door. "Just leave it alone."

Pearl was sound asleep by nine o'clock, exhausted and worn out by angry tears. Winnie stared at her sleeping face, wondering at her sister's rage, the overwhelming power of her fury. Pearl would survive no matter what happened. She would survive through the sheer strength of her own will.

Winnie walked to the bedroom window, opened it as wide as it would go, stepped out onto the steep-pitched roof and sat down. It was her favourite place in this dark and dreary house, the one place she could feel what she'd felt as a child, small and free beneath an endless stretch of sky that bent down to embrace an endless horizon. The sunset was a miracle of hot pink strata tonight, edged in yellow and mauve, blending into the wide open blue. She could see beyond the rooftops of town, to the flat prairie where her father had tried to scrabble out a living. Now lush and golden with crops, it had once been nothing more than blowing dirt. And the dust had settled over everything: their clothing, their food, her father's heart.

Winnie had always known how her aunt and uncle felt about her, but now that it had been put into words, she felt relief. She owed them nothing, and there was nothing keeping her here except Pearl.

Winnie unrolled her spine against the warm shingles of the roof and stared at the darkening sky. Life was a bitter pill sometimes. You either hurt the people you loved or you hurt yourself. And she was so tired of living in pain.

On Friday night, when her aunt and uncle left to play cards with the neighbours, Winnie lifted her suitcase onto the bed, opened the lid and began filling it, first with her underwear, then sweaters and shirts and finally her denim overalls and two good pairs of pants. She stared into the closet at the dresses her aunt had made for her and the navy blue pleated tunics she wore to school. *Those can stay*, she thought as she closed the closet door and walked over to her night table. She opened the drawer and pulled out the keepsakes she'd taken from the farm: her father's beat-up silver pocket watch, her mother's sewing shears, her brother's book and letters. The shears were beautiful, silver and gold, with a filigree pattern etched down the length of the blades, and they were sharp enough to cut through tin. Winnie had always admired them the way she admired any useful, well-designed tool. She was wrapping them in a piece of cloth when Pearl walked in.

"What are you doing?" she asked.

"I'm leaving," Winnie said.

"Well, you're not going without me." Pearl strode across the room, got down on her hands and knees and pulled her own suitcase out from under the bed. "You've got another think coming if you think I'm going to stay in this house with the two of them."

"You can't come," Winnie said.

"The hell I can't." Pearl walked over to the dresser and pulled out a handful of panties.

"Sit down," Winnie said.

Pearl ignored her and stuffed the underwear into her case. Winnie walked over, grabbed her by the shoulders and pushed her down to the bed.

"You're not leaving, Pearl. You're only fifteen. You have to finish school."

"You haven't finished school yet, and I don't give a good goddamn about it," she shouted into her sister's face. "I want to be with you."

"Well, you can't. I don't even have a place to stay, and if you come now, we'll both be on the street. Just wait until Joe gets back from overseas. Then you can leave."

Pearl shook her head and pounded her fists on her knees. "But I can't stay with them. They hate me. And I hate them."

"You have to stay, Pearl. There's no other choice. If I find a place, maybe then, but for right now you have to stay put."

"It's that goddamned farm, isn't it? You can't have it, so you're leaving me. You're leaving me all alone."

"That's not true. I just don't belong here. I don't really belong anywhere."

"You belong with me," Pearl said, getting to her feet. "And if you leave, I swear to God, I'll never speak to you again, Winnie. I'll disown you. You'll never be my sister again."

Winnie stared at the floor. "I never was your sister, Pearl."

Winnie could hear the sound of running, heard the bedroom door slam shut, heard the pounding of her little sister's feet as they raced down the stairs.

"And I was never anybody's daughter."

Jolene's one-room apartment was located above the Nighthawk Diner, and the hallway always smelt of food. Tonight, it smelled like the evening specials: sausages and sauerkraut, liver, bacon and onions. Downstairs in the restaurant, someone turned up the radio. The soft strains of *Moonlight Serenade* echoed up the stairwell, matching Winnie's steps as she trudged up the stairs and knocked on the door.

Jolene answered, wearing a red and yellow flowered dress with a white patent leather belt cinched tight at the waist, and her toes peeked out from the front of her high-heeled shoes, shoes that were chalky white, thick with many coats of carefully applied polish. Her smile faded as she opened the door.

"Winnie," she said. "What are you doing here?"

"I left home. I was wondering if you could put me up for the night."

"Gosh, Winnie, there's not much room and I'm expecting a visitor," Jolene said, peering around the edge of the door and down the stairs.

"Sure. That's okay, Jolene. I'll try hitching a ride out of town with one of the guys downstairs."

"Don't do that." Jolene sighed. "They're all perverts downstairs tonight. Come on inside and tell me what happened."

Once they settled in, Winnie told her the story and Jolene shook her head. "Could be worse. You could have been born into my family."

Winnie stared at the floor. Everybody in town knew about Jolene's family, just like they knew about Winnie's mother and father. They knew that Jolene's father had died, and her mother had married a man who drank too much and worked her two kids like dray horses. And there were rumours about other things as well, darker things between Jolene and her stepfather that the local women spoke about in hushed voices. Her aunt called Jolene a little slut, but then her aunt called most young girls by nasty names.

"Have you heard from your brother lately?" Winnie asked.

Jolene smiled. "Henry writes me every week. He's still in England, but he thinks there'll be another landing soon."

"I hope to God they don't land at Dieppe again."

Jolene sighed. "I liked your brother, you know. Mattie was always nice to me. Real nice."

"If only he'd made it," Winnie said, her eyes tearing up. "If he'd lived, everything would have been different. He would have come home to run the farm, and I would have helped him."

"Mattie wouldn't want you to be alone, Winnie. Come to the dance tomorrow night and get yourself a nice young farmer. You can still have what you want. You'll see."

Winnie's tears flowed freely now, tears for her dead brother and her little sister, for her mother and father and for herself and the lovely Jolene, who stared back at her with only kindness and compassion in her eyes.

"She'll get over it," Jolene said. "Pearl's a hothead, but she'll forgive you."

"No," Winnie replied. "I don't think she will."

Before she could finish, there was a knock at the door, and Jolene ran to answer it. Everything after that happened in a kind of blur. Jolene introducing her to a young man in a sharp-pressed blue serge uniform, the two of them swirling out the door on their way to the Starlight movie theatre, Jolene's arm wound around his.

"I won't be late," she called back as the door clicked shut behind them.

At eight o'clock that evening, Winnie reached the highway that led out of town. She decided she had nothing left to lose, so she had written Jolene a note explaining everything: who she was, what she wanted, whom she loved. Maybe Jolene would burn the note, or maybe she'd hold it next to her heart and keep it close to her always. Winnie wouldn't know, and she didn't want to know, because she didn't want to break her own heart. It was broken enough already.

She set her case down on the shoulder of the road and sat down to wait. Five minutes later a truck showed-up, its flat bed filled with a dozen fly boys on their way back to the base. When the driver spotted her, he rolled to a halt, and two young pilots pulled the pins on the loading door. It dropped with a hollow bang, and their hands reached out, offering to pull her in. Winnie stared up at their grinning faces, hesitated, then decided that she didn't really care. She put out her hands, allowed herself to be lifted in, and the truck lurched forward.

"Where are you off to?" one of them asked.

"Home," she said. "To my parents' farm."

"Sure you wouldn't like to come up to the base with us and have some fun?" one of them asked, leering at her, pressing his body close to hers. The other men laughed at his boldness and crowded in around her. Winnie didn't stop to consider the consequences. She just turned around, kneed the boy closest to her, and he fell to the floor of the truck, clutching his groin.

Two of his buddies bent down to commiserate, and Winnie turned to face the others. "Anyone else want to try?" she asked.

They all stared at her, stared at the small, square olive-skinned girl with the fierce dark eyes, strong arms and black hair. She could feel their anger building, sense the threat in them. Then a tall blond boy started to laugh, and one by one they all joined in.

"Not bad for a girl," said the tall boy.

Winnie smiled darkly. "Who said I was a girl?" she asked, and they laughed even louder.

As they drove down the highway, Winnie spoke with each of them in turn, learning their names, where they came from and what their dreams were. They came from across the country and all over the world: the blond boy, Victor, came from Chicago, Bennie and Cliff from Vancouver, and Allan Peters all the way from Australia. She told them about her brother, Mattie, who had died at Dieppe, and they listened, silent. By the time they reached the dirt road that led to the farm, Winnie felt as if she were one of them. Everything about them made sense to her: their hard laughter and bravado, their big hands, the silence that spoke of what they felt but could not say.

Are you sure you'll be all right?" Victor asked as she climbed out of the truck. "It looks pretty deserted."

"I'll be fine. Thanks for the ride. And sorry about that," she said to the boy she'd kneed, but he frowned and turned away.

As the truck lurched forward again, each man raised a hand. They didn't wave, just held them there, as if they had been frozen in time. Most of them would soon be dead, as dead as her parents and her brother.

The door of the abandoned farmhouse was closed, but it wasn't locked, so Winnie walked inside, and as she made her way through the house, she could feel the ghosts pressing in on her. The ghost of her mother who had died at her father's hands, and her father who had died at his own – a man who had screamed for help every night of his life, screamed from a wasteland of blasted trees where no life grew, the distant battleground where he'd lost his heart and most of his life. Her mother was half dead from cancer when her father put that pillow over her face and smothered her. And there was little doubt that he had been half dead too when he walked away from her and hanged himself in the barn. But Pearl didn't know any of that, because Winnie had never told her. At first, Pearl had been too young to understand. Then she had become too angry to listen.

Winnie stood in the empty kitchen and stared down at a pair of work boots that sat next to the kitchen door, their toes curled back with age, the cotton laces little more than mouse-eaten shreds. Winnie had followed her father around like a puppy dog, because she wanted to be like her father; she had wanted to be her father, even though she knew that he only had eyes for Pearl, because Pearl was everything a little girl should be. Even though he had sometimes struck their mother, even though he'd whipped Matthew within an inch of his life, he had never struck Pearl. And he'd only hit Winnie once, right across her face, with the full force of his open hand.

"Call me Will, Daddy," she'd said. "I'm Will, just like you."

Winnie set her case down on the porch that wrapped itself around the doorway and down the length of the grey plank walls. She opened the lid, picked up her mother's cloth-wrapped shears and went down the stairs, past the barn, following the path that led to the creek. Near the water, she sat down on a rock, unwrapped the shears and stared at them. Then she reached around her neck, pulled her plaited hair forward and cut it off at the base. She walked to the edge of the creek and threw it in. The plait of black hair floated on the surface of the water then slowly sank.

CHAPTER 4

2000

At eight thirty on Friday morning, Carol walked out the front door and picked up the newspaper. A fresh pot of coffee was brewing, Nathan was on his way to work and her two grown-up sons had left for the weekend. Finally, she was free to do what she loved to do.

Every Friday for the past two months, Carol had been repeating this ritual. She'd skim the front page of the newspaper and clip whatever coupons looked interesting off the back page. Then she'd comb the want ads. Today, she was looking for a dining room suite, so she would check the antiques section as well. She was tired of that black lacquered set. It was only five years old and already out of date, whereas antiques never aged. They just appreciated in value.

Over the past year, Carol had become an *Antiques Roadshow* fanatic, although she preferred the British version to the American one. The Brits were so much more reserved, their experts so enthusiastically eccentric. Even when they were being a bit snotty, they were charming, unlike most of the American experts, who looked like sharks. And all the people who appeared on camera looked as if they had dollar signs ka-chinging in their eyes. All except for that one old man, the one with his father's folk art carvings that turned out to be worth a fortune. When he found out, his eyes had filled with tears and so had Carol's, because the man reminded her of her father: kindhearted and poor.

Well, her father might have been poor, but she'd given him a lovely funeral, with long-stemmed white roses and white calla lilies on his casket and a beautiful bronze urn for his ashes. The only blot on the event had been her mother, dressed in that horrible dress, with her big breasts and her ham-hock arms bursting it at the seams. Carol had offered to buy her a new dress, but as usual her mother had refused.

"I don't need a new dress to bury my husband any more than he needs a four-thousand-dollar casket," Pearl said, stomping into the kitchen to slice up yet another roll of those soggy pinwheel sandwiches for the funeral tea: deviled ham with a dill pickle in the middle, cream cheese with a fluorescent cherry, tuna fish with a pimento heart.

Carol sipped her coffee. Why in God's name had her father married her mother?

Carol stared at the front page of the paper and decided to skip the news and the coupons. It wasn't as if she'd learn anything new by reading yet another article about American politics, and it wasn't as if she didn't have enough money to buy her dishwasher detergent full price. So she got out her soft red pencil, pulled out the classifieds and turned to her favourite section: Household Items.

"Household contents. Everything must go. Fridge,

stove, brand new bedroom suite and much more."

Carol stared at the ad. There was a story there, she was sure: maybe a divorce or a transfer. Perhaps someone had lost a job and was selling out. Or maybe an old lady had died, and the kids were selling off her possessions and splitting up the proceeds.

Carol shivered. Just the thought of going through her mother's things made her feel a bit queasy. She couldn't imagine selling any of it. None of it was worth anything. Everything her mother owned was old and worn out and smelled of stale pipe smoke and Pine-Sol, overlaid with the nauseating odour of Irish Spring soap.

Carol turned back to the newspaper. The next five ads were for various types of exercise equipment: rowing machines, bike machines, machines with weights and treadmills. The same kind of machines were gathering dust in Carol's basement, so she skipped those. She also skipped over three fridges, two stoves, one all-wood bedroom suite – no specific wood noted – and a vintage 1960s kitchen table and chairs until she finally found what she was looking for:

"Antique Gibbard dining room suite: three leaves, eight chairs, buffet and china cabinet. $6000."

Well, the price was a bit steep. Maybe she should just circle the ad and keep looking. Two paragraphs down, she read another ad and stopped dead.

"For sale, two mother-of-the-bride dresses. Size 12."

Carol stared at the telephone number at the bottom of the ad and lowered her coffee cup onto the table. She stood up so fast that she almost knocked over her chair in her rush to get to the phone. She grabbed the receiver and dialed her sister's number. On the sixth ring, Darlene finally answered.

"Hello," she said, her voice dozy with sleep.

"Darlene, it's Carol."

"Carol, Jesus. It's eight thirty. What's going on?"

"Mother. That's what's going on, Darlene. Did you read the classifieds this morning?"

"Carol, it's eight thirty. I'm barely awake. And besides, the classifieds are your thing, not mine."

"She's selling our wedding dresses. Can you believe that? She's actually selling our wedding dresses."

"What are you talking about? I threw mine out years ago."

"No, Darlene. Not *our* wedding dresses. Her *mother-of-the-bride dresses*."

There was a guffaw at the other end of the line. "Oh, for Christ's sake, Carol, those dresses are thirty years old. No one's going to buy them. And besides, who cares?" Darlene said in that irritatingly patronizing tone she took when responding to anything that Carol deemed important.

"I care," she said, trying to suppress the whine in her voice and failing. "Don't you see what she's doing?"

"No, Carol. I don't."

"It's her way of punishing us. It's a slap in the face, that's what it is."

"Only if you give a shit, and I don't. Now, if you don't mind, I was up late last night, and I haven't even had my coffee yet. So I'm hanging up now."

The line went dead and Carol was left staring at the receiver. She put it down on its cradle, picked it up again, hesitated a few seconds, then dialed. The phone rang three times, a message machine cut in, and her mother's voice boomed across the line.

"Is this thing working, Henry? Henry! Oh, hell, just leave us a message and I'll try to figure it out."

Carol hung up the phone in the middle of the message beep and trudged back to the kitchen table. She picked up the mug with the big blue letters spelling out her name and downed the rest of her coffee in one swig. She stared out the kitchen window at her lovely weed-less lawn and the little bed of wilted marigolds that sat there, mocking her, by dying in the shade of the crab apple tree.

"What in God's name are you doing?" her mother had asked as she lumbered into the back yard.

Once again, Pearl had dropped by unannounced, and Carol could feel herself tense. "Why didn't you call, Mom? I have to go out in half an hour."

"Oh, never mind that. I wasn't planning on staying all day. Now, what are you doing?" she said, pointing at the flat of marigolds that sat on the grass next to Carol.

"I'm planting marigolds," Carol said and turned back to the bed under the crab apple tree. "They remind me of Dad."

Her mother folded her arms. "Well, I don't know why they remind you of your father. I'm the one who always planted them. And you shouldn't be putting them there. Marigolds need sun. They'll die in all that shade."

Carol bristled. "It is sunny here. In fact, this is the sunniest part of the yard," she lied.

"Well, far be it from me to tell you what to do. After all, what do I know? I've only been planting the same god-damned marigolds for the last fifty years."

Carol hacked at the roots of the crab apple tree with her spade. "Why don't you go into the house and get a cup of coffee, Mom? It's in the pot next to the stove."

Carol stared out the window at the spindly, flowerless marigolds. Why did it always go like that? Why did her mother always manage to make her feel as if she were the one who had done something wrong? Now Pearl was selling her mother-of-the-bride dress, and she knew damn well that Carol would find the ad. It was her way of saying, "To hell with you." Her way of saying that she was getting rid of a bad daughter and a lot of bad memories.

Carol straightened her shoulders. That ad was the last straw. There would be no more Sunday dinners and no more family get-togethers. No more listening to her mother's coarse language and constant criticism. If she phoned, Carol simply wouldn't answer. After all, the main reason she had visited her mother was to see her father, and now that he was dead, she didn't have to keep up the pretense any more.

Carol put her empty cup down, swept the newspaper off the kitchen table, strode back to the telephone and dialed. It rang three times and a woman answered.

"Yes, hello," Carol said. "I'm calling about your ad for the dining room suite? Yes. Yes, I would like to see it. Tomorrow at ten? Sure, that would be fine. 484 Catcher's Drive. Yes, I know it. Thank you. See you then."

Carol hung up the phone, impressed. Catcher's Drive was one of the swankiest streets in the city. So why was the woman selling the table? Carol walked over to the utility closet and pulled out the vacuum hose. Maybe she needed the money, maybe her husband was dead or perhaps he'd divorced her. Or maybe he'd jilted her for a younger woman.

Carol sighed as she shoved the hose into the wall outlet and vacuumed up the toast crumbs from underneath the kitchen table. That was probably it. Men with too much money were always doing that sort of thing. Her own husband, Nathan, made good money, but he wasn't what you'd call rich: comfortable, yes, but not rich. So Nathan would never leave her for a younger woman, because he couldn't afford to even if he wanted to, which he never would.

At five thirty that evening, Carol set a lovely table for two and lit some candles, but when Nathan got home from work, he rushed into the family room and turned on the VCR.

"The second round of the Open was on this afternoon, and I taped it," he called out to her. "Let's get the TV tables and eat in here."

"But the table's set, Nathan. Can't you wait until we eat?"

"Oh, come on, Carol. It's just the two of us. If you want to eat at the table, go ahead. I'll just eat in here."

Carol hated eating in front of the TV, but she didn't want to eat alone again, so she blew out the candles and carried their plates into the family room. As she dabbed up the last of her spaghetti sauce with a piece of garlic toast and washed it down with a mouthful of wine, she watched Nathan watching the TV. At least he was easy to please. She glanced at the golf game. Tiger Woods was lining up for his next putt. He tapped the ball, and Carol watched as it rolled slowly down the green and stopped right on the lip of the cup. It hovered there for what seemed like forever then suddenly pitched forward and dropped into the hole. The crowd in California cheered, and so did Nathan.

"Did you see that?" he shouted. "That kid can't do anything wrong."

Carol smiled and decided to share her own good news. "Oh, Nathan, I almost forgot to tell you. I think I found the dining room suite I've been looking for."

"Good for you," he said, his eyes still glued to the TV.

"Well, it's six thousand dollars. A bit more than I wanted to spend."

"Whatever you want." The crowd cheered again, and Nathan banged his hands on the TV table. "This is going to be close, really close. I just hope the guys I'm golfing with tomorrow are watching this."

"So what do you think? Is six thousand too much?"

"Too much for what, Carol?"

"For the dining room suite. Do you think it's too expensive?"

"Jesus. Can't we talk about this later?"

Carol picked up her utensils, balanced her wine glass on her plate and walked over to collect Nathan's dirty dishes. "I just thought you might be interested, that's all," she said as she picked up his plate.

Nathan hit the pause button and sighed. "You know I leave that stuff to you. Buy whatever you want. How many times do I have to tell you that? Besides, I'm sure the table will be great."

Carol nodded, and Nathan hit play. The announcer whispered into the microphone, "This is the shot that could make or break this tournament, ladies and gentlemen."

There was a moment of silence. Then the crowd moaned, and Nathan cheered. A player he wasn't rooting for must have missed his shot.

Carol closed the kitchen door with her foot and put the dirty dishes on the counter. She carried her wine glass over to the bottle that sat on the kitchen table, but it was empty, so she walked over to the fridge and pulled out a new one.

She opened it and filled her glass. Between sips, she flipped down the door of her new dishwasher and loaded it with the dirty dishes. When she was finished, she walked over to the kitchen window and stared at the dying marigolds.

Tomorrow she would dig them up and throw them away. Then she'd buy some new ones and plant them in a different spot.

The next morning, after Nathan left for his golf game, Carol pulled her brand new sundress off its pink satin hanger. It was such a pretty dress, yellow with little blue butterflies scattered across it. She took her white strapped sandals off the shoe rack, buckled them on and transferred her wallet, keys and cosmetics from her fake Gucci purse to her white leather shoulder bag. She smoothed her dress over her hips and smiled at herself in the mirror. Her hair was clean and shiny, and her nails were painted a gorgeous frosted blue. Her legs were waxed, her eyebrows plucked, and she felt as light as a feather. She felt like a million bucks.

She walked out of the bedroom and headed down the stairs. If she'd known she would feel this good, she would have gotten rid of her mother years ago. Halfway down, she stopped and looked over the railing into the living room. Her friends said that she had a real flair for room design, and Carol was inclined to agree. She loved this room. Loved the clean, off-white walls, the pink love seats, the chintz covered armchairs and the swag curtains held back by the big eight-inch Roman coins. What a find they'd been, on sale at La Lampe for just seventy dollars.

Carol stepped down off the last stair and headed through the kitchen to the door that led to her two-car garage. The phone rang, and she stopped at the kitchen counter to look at the call display box. It was her mother's number.

Let it ring, she thought, and pulled the answering machine cord out of the wall. She would wait until her mother gave up. Then she'd plug the machine back in. But the phone just kept ringing. Six rings. Eight rings. Finally, on the tenth ring, her mother hung up. Carol slipped the answering machine plug back into the wall and hesitated. What if her mother called again? What if she left a message?

Carol steeled herself for the inevitable. Even if her mother did leave a message, it didn't mean she had to call her back. Her mind was made up. So when her cell phone suddenly rang, and she fished it out of her purse to find her sister's number flashing on the screen, she turned it off. She didn't want to talk to Darlene any more than she wanted to talk to her mother. Why ruin a perfectly good day with more snide remarks? Besides, she had a new project to think about. She was going to buy that Gibbard suite then repaint the dining room. Maybe she'd even change the wall-to-wall. She'd seen a sample for a fabulous deep-purple pile. Maybe she'd buy that.

Carol stuffed her cell phone back into her purse, walked to the garage, got into her brand new Toyota Corolla, pressed the automatic door opener and backed out down the drive. Twenty minutes later, she turned left off Callingwood onto Weaver's Lane, then right onto Catcher's Drive. 484, the woman had said. She passed 396, a school-sized split level from the 1960s. 415 was a modern monstrosity with a cement façade and a ton of those glass bricks forming a semi-circular entryway on the side. At 443, the houses started to change. The lots were bigger, and the homes looked like country estates. Carol rolled her car to a stop opposite one of them. She turned off the engine, got out of the car, stepped up onto the curb and stood on her tiptoes, straining to see over the massive hedge that encircled the palatial yard at the front of the house. The building was enormous, built of limestone just like the legislature, and it even had turrets and a sweeping circular drive.

Carol rearranged the straps on her sundress. This kind of ostentatious wealth just annoyed her. As if anyone really needed that much space. It was just silly, she decided as she hoisted her purse over her shoulder. Walking across the street and up the endless drive, she finally arrived at the front door. When she rang the bell, a Filipino woman in a smart red dress answered.

"Can I help you?"

"Yes," Carol replied, suddenly feeling much more confidant. "We spoke yesterday. I've come to see your dining room suite. The one that's for sale?"

"Oh. You'll want Mrs. Tipperton, then. Please, come in," the woman said, sweeping the heavy gothic door open to let Carol inside.

Carol stepped across the threshold into an oak paneled hallway. Opposite her was a broad circular staircase, and above her head was a vast vaulted ceiling. Carol stared up at the ornate festoons that looped around small plaster cherubs and panicked.

What had she gotten herself into?

She turned around to make her excuses and flee, but the woman who had answered the door was nowhere in sight. By the time she turned back to the staircase, another woman had materialized on the second floor landing. She wore white linen pants and a loose silk shirt the colour of cappuccino. Her earrings were huge, solid gold hoops, and on her wrists were two heavy chain-link bracelets made of the same gold. Her hair was a perfect helmet of silver and grey, the bangs perfectly trimmed, the blunt edges that brushed her cheeks, cut to sway, just as they had swayed in high school.

Carol stared at the woman descending the stairs and clutched her purse. It was Eileen Collins. It was Eileen bloody Collins.

"Eileen Tipperton," the woman said, silently gliding down the last three stairs and extending her hand.

Carol reached out for Eileen's long, bony fingers. "Carol Bukowski."

Except for the grey hair and the last name, Eileen looked exactly the same: perfect teeth, perfect skin, perfect eyes and thin as a toothpick. Carol fingered one of her butterfly earrings and braced herself for the moment of recognition.

Eileen looked just to the right of Carol's head. "How nice. Well, the room where we keep the Gibbard suite is right through here, Carol. Ordinarily I'd have Maria show you the table, but this is my grandmother's dining room suite, and I want to make sure it's going to a good home. Just follow me," she said, taking the lead in her soft, flat, calfskin leather shoes.

Carol stared down at her own feet clamped tight in their Cuban heeled sandals, the thin white straps cutting into the flesh of her big toe. She clomped across the hardwood floor behind Eileen.

They walked through the first living room then through a second living room. They walked through a library filled with shelf upon shelf of leather bound books and into a dining room, where Carol got her first glimpse of a real set of French provincial furniture: a massive table, fifteen chairs and a sideboard the size of her two-car garage. On the sideboard and table were huge sprays of freshly cut flowers: masses of blue delphiniums and a riot of red and pink and cream flowers Carol didn't recognize.

"You're selling this?" she gasped.

Eileen's laughter tinkled off the chandelier. "Oh heavens, no. We keep the one I'm selling in our everyday dining room off the kitchen." She swept her arm to the side as if she were Jacqueline Kennedy leading a tour of the White House. "My husband, Tip, is tired of it and wants something more modern that doesn't watermark. And there's this wonderful little furniture designer in town. Perhaps you know him – Zen Walko?"

"No, I don't think I do," Carol said.

Eileen stared at her French-tipped nails. "His things are wonderful, very unique. So I said to Tip, 'Let's get one of Zen's pieces.'" She smiled at Carol. "His work is very reasonable."

"It is?"

"Oh God, yes. Twenty thousand is incredibly reasonable for an original design. Now," she said, pushing open two French doors to reveal a creamy sunlit room with floor-to-ceiling windows that overlooked the river. "Here we are. This is my grandmother's suite."

Carol could feel Eileen's eyes following her as she stepped forward, her Cuban heels clattering across the marble floor like a pair of castanets. The table was beautiful, with delicate legs and a rich, dark brown surface. Beside it sat a small buffet and china cabinet with the most exquisite scrollwork behind its glass doors.

"Cute, isn't it?" Eileen said.

"Yes," Carol said without thinking. "It's beautiful." Then she made the mistake of looking up, straight into Eileen's blinking, birdlike eyes.

"Wait a minute," Eileen said, her eyes narrowing to slits. "I know you from somewhere, don't I?"

"Oh, really?" Carol said, fighting to keep the panic out of her voice.

"Maybe we met at one of Tip's political events?"

"Oh, no, I don't think so," Carol said. "I don't really participate in politics."

As soon as the words were out of her mouth, Carol instantly regretted them. *I don't participate in politics.* It made her sound as if she didn't even vote, and she did vote, but it was too late to explain that to Eileen Tipperton. Her eyes were already glazing over.

"Oh, well, never mind. I'm sure I'll think of it," Eileen said, turning her attention back to the matter at hand. "So, are you interested in the table?"

Carol decided that the only way out was to lie. "Actually, I was looking for something just a bit bigger."

"Oh," Eileen said, her eyes snapping shut and open again. "Well, I'll have Maria show you out. Maria!" Eileen shouted. "Maria, where are you?"

When no answer came, she turned back to Carol with a look of bored impatience. "I suppose I'll have to show you out, then."

Carol turned to follow Eileen back through her extravagant home, feeling like a tradesman who'd done a bit of shoddy work and was now being summarily dismissed. She desperately wanted to say something witty and rude, but when they reached the front door, she found herself apologizing.

"I'm sorry for the inconvenience," she said, staring at the floor. "It really is a lovely table."

When she looked up again, Eileen's eyes were wide with a look of sudden recognition.

"I've got it," she said, clapping her hands together. "I know who you are! You're Carol Calder, aren't you? The girl they transferred into the gifted class in grade eleven. Of course, that's who you are. And you went out with Phil Paxton, didn't you? Oh God, we were all so jealous," she said, flashing the same superior smile she'd always smiled when gliding through the halls of Courtland High, surrounded by her entourage of hangers on.

The smile vanished, and Eileen raised a French-tipped finger to her lips, her face a mask of mock perturbation. "And, oh dear. You got pregnant at the end of grade twelve, didn't you, Carol?" she said, her lips curving back into a viciously thin smile. "Well, that certainly took Phil out of circulation, now, didn't it?"

Carol felt as if she could actually hear the ground shift under her feet. Her face burned to a hot red, and humiliation surged up the back of her legs and into her groin. Her first thought was to bolt and run rather than give this woman the satisfaction of seeing her cry. Instead, she felt her mouth open and heard her mother's voice booming out from the back of her head. And like a clairvoyant taken by the spirit, Carol took a sharp breath in and stood straight up. Her head shot back and her breast thrust forward against her yellow and blue butterfly sundress, and for the first time in thirty years, the words in Carol's head shot out of her mouth and into the air.

"Jesus Christ, Eileen. You always were a bitch. And by God, you still are," she said.

And with her words still crackling in the air between them, Carol turned away from the house at 484 Catcher's Drive and away from the woman she had always imagined she wanted to be. And as she marched down Eileen's circular driveway, she heard her father's voice, heard it clear as a bell: "You're just like your mother, Carol. Full of piss and vinegar. Full of spunk."

And where the hell had all that spunk gone? How many times since Phil Paxton had climbed onto his motorcycle and run it into that concrete road divider had she sat on her tongue, sat on her anger, sat on what she really felt in her heart?

He'd been home no more than an hour when he announced that he was leaving again.

"Please don't go," Carol pleaded as she followed him down the hallway of their tiny apartment. She had Jason in one arm and Daniel held fast to her pant leg. Phil grabbed his helmet and gloves from the floor where he'd tossed them, flung open the door and walked out.

"I hate you," she shouted.

The door slammed shut behind him, and both boys started to cry.

Two hours later, when the police arrived to tell her what had happened, they hadn't been able to explain it. The road had been empty, they said. There didn't appear to be anything wrong with his motorcycle. Maybe he'd swerved to miss an animal. Maybe he'd been going so fast, he just lost control of the bike.

"I want a divorce," he said when he finally woke up and found her sitting in his hospital room. "You can have the kids. I don't want them. And I don't want you."

When Carol told her mother what had happened, Pearl just shook her head. "Good riddance. I always said he was a useless son of a bitch."

Carol opened her car door and fell into the driver's seat.

Why hadn't her mother been kind? Why hadn't she been just a bit more sympathetic? Carol's heart had been broken when Phillip left, but something else inside her had been broken too, and her mother didn't seem to see that. She didn't seem to care. All her mother had ever cared about was being right.

"And another thing," Pearl had said, shaking a gloved finger in Carol's face. "Just because you're pregnant doesn't mean you have to marry that boy. You can give the baby up for adoption or raise it at home with us. That boy is bad news, Carol. Mark my words. He's bad news."

They'd been standing at the bus stop just outside the Medical Arts building in the freezing cold for more than fifteen minutes. The snow drove down in angled sheets, and her mother was bent against the wind, but Carol stood tall and warm, wrapped inside the old raccoon coat she'd bought at the thrift store. Old fur coats were all the rage at school, and this one had been a great find. Heavy and long with broad, stiff shoulder pads, it hung in folds, draping down her body to just below her knees. But more importantly, the coat was nice and wide: wide enough to hide her body and the thing that was growing inside.

"Well," the doctor said. "The tests are positive, Carol. You're pregnant, all right, about three months. Do you have any questions?

Carol shook her head.

Her mother groaned. "Jesus," she said, staring at the green and black tiled floor. "What do we do now?"

"Nothing," the doctor said. "Just make an appointment for next month and come back in. In the meantime, make sure she eats well. And get lots of sleep, Carol. No more running around," he said with a leering smile.

Her mother grunted to her feet, her gaze still fixed on the floor. "Well, come on, then, Carol. The man hasn't got all day. I need to get you home."

As her mother walked out, Carol could feel the doctor staring at her, looking at her miniskirt, watching her as she pulled on her raccoon coat.

"Quite the getup," he said and shook his head. "No big surprise you wound up pregnant."

Carol just stood there and watched him as he got up from his chair and walked out the side door into the next examining room. As he closed the door, she could hear him greet his next patient.

"Ah, Mrs. Davies. Pregnant again, are we? You naughty girl."

"He said what?" her mother asked as the elevator lurched into motion.

Carol glanced at the strange man standing in the far corner of the elevator and tried to shush her mother.

"Don't you dare shush me. Get over there and press eight. We're going back up."

"No," Carol whispered. "I don't want to go back up there. I just want to go home."

"I'm telling you right now," her mother hissed, shaking her finger in Carol's face. "When I get you home, I'm calling that man. Give him a good piece of my mind. And we're not going back there, either. We'll find another doctor."

"Whatever," Carol said, shrugging her shoulders and turning to face the elevator door.

As the carriage bounced to a stop, she heard her mother sigh. "Although that thing is a bit ratty," she said, tugging on the back of Carol's coat.

Carol could feel tears stinging at the corner of her eyes as she marched out of the elevator and through the lobby toward the front door of the Medical Arts Building.

"Oh, for God's sake, Carol, don't be so damned sensitive," her mother called out after her. "I didn't say he was right. I just think you need a new coat."

When they got to the bus stop, Carol turned to look at her mother, who had turned to look down the street to see if the bus was coming. She looked at the old mohair coat her mother had worn for as long as she could remember, at her knitted blue hat, her worn leather gloves and the flat-heeled, zippered boots that didn't quite fit over her thick, muscled calves.

Is that the way they thought she should dress? Is that the way you dressed if you didn't want to get pregnant? If it were, then Carol would be pregnant for the rest of her life, because she would never dress like her mother. She would never be like her mother. Never in a million years.

In the end, Philip had married her at the eleventh hour, just before the baby was born. Carol had been as shocked as anyone, because it was Phil who had suggested it. Right out of the blue, him sitting on his motorcycle, her leaning against the back fence: "We might as well get married," he said, and that was that.

At the time, she'd been over the moon, but looking back it all made a perverse kind of sense. Philip had married her to spite his wealthy parents, but even that hadn't worked, because they refused to come to the wedding. It had been a small, somber affair, with only her stone-faced mother, her father and sister, a minister and a photographer in attendance. Not one member of Phil's family had shown up, and it was so last minute that there wasn't any time to invite their friends. When the ceremony was over, they all had dinner at a fine dining restaurant, paid for by Carol's father. Then the two of them had driven back to their tiny bachelor apartment. As soon as he walked in the door, Phillip had whipped off his tie, peeled off his suit and climbed into his leathers.

"Thank God that's over." He grinned at her and kissed the top of her head. "Time to go to work."

Just before the door clicked shut behind him, he called back to her. "Catch you later, Carol."

And that was what she had spent the next five years trying to do: catch Phil, pin him down, turn him into a husband and a father.

And where had that gotten her? Carol wondered.

Gripping the Toyota's steering wheel, she pushed her back against the driver's seat and stared out the window. The long, straight boulevards of Catcher's Drive stretched out in front of her. It looked as if someone had lit the grass and sliced the edges of the houses with a straight razor. Two houses down, a man in a straw hat turned on a mower and began sheering the lawn into straight rows of alternating shades of green. Behind her a car door slammed, and Carol glanced into the rear-view mirror. A woman was walking to the back of her car. She opened the trunk and began unloading shopping bags, their brightly coloured logos advertising their origins: the Bay and Eaton's, Safeway and Sears. She watched the woman trudge up her walk, her arms straining under the weight of her burden.

Carol closed her eyes. How many years had she spent allowing people to treat her as if she were just so much shit on a sales clerk's shoe? As if she were a scatter-brained moron who had to be tolerated? Even her sons treated her as if she didn't have a brain in her head, making fun of her when she forgot things at the grocery store, like the shaving cream they should have been buying for themselves. She'd given up everything to make a life for those two boys, and they had no business treating her like a maid with a low IQ. And neither did Nathan. All Nathan ever did was sigh. Sigh when she was excited about a new wall colour. Sigh when she made a new recipe. Sigh when she cried in bed, because he'd rejected her for the ninety-ninth time. Sigh when what she really wanted was a man who would hold her in his arms and tell her that her life hadn't been a total waste of time.

Carol jammed her key into the ignition and started her car. There would be no more sighing from Nathan, no more smart-ass remarks from her sons and absolutely no more bullshit from her mother. So what if she'd planted her marigolds in the wrong spot? She deserved some respect, and from now on, she was going to get it.

She cranked the key in the ignition and was about to pull away from the curb when her cell phone rang again. She flipped it open, saw the number on the display screen and decided that her sister was as good a place to start as any.

"What?" she barked, and as she listened, Carol's newly righted world began to tilt again.

CHAPTER 5

2000

The sign on the building said Hôtel Dieu, and there it sat like a great Gothic hotel: God's Hotel. A 420-bed hospital in the heart of downtown. Too bad it wasn't the Sheraton. At least then she could have had a decent cup of coffee and worked on her paper without all this moaning, without this "suffer the little children to come unto me" attitude.

"Your mother's resting comfortably," the perky little nurse had said. "She's a real little peach."

Darlene would have preferred the callous admitting-room stereotype to this cloying grade school approach. Her mother, Pearl, was not little, nor was she a peach. Her mother was like her name: like sand between your toes, an irritant that had rolled itself into something hard and round and opaque but not smooth. More like a freshwater pearl: irregular and covered in ridges.

Maybe that's why Darlene was so obsessed with Mary, Mother of God, the virgin wife and mother. She was every-thing Pearl was not – the perfect picture of unconditional love and nurturance, the perfect woman for sexually challenged church fathers. You didn't even have to touch her and she did what she was supposed to do: get pregnant and bear the Son of God, the man with the big ideas. Odd how the substandard gender could always symbolize the good stuff. Like the Statue of Liberty, they could give birth to a great idea, but they couldn't actually hold one in their heads.

Just like her sister, Carol. The girl voted most likely to succeed in high school, Carol had turned her brain off in 1972 and had never turned it back on again. And where was Carol now, when Darlene really needed her? Probably out buying something or getting her hair done.

Sometimes Darlene felt remorse when she treated her sister like an idiot, but most of the time she just couldn't help herself. It enraged her to see Carol wasting her life on interior decorating and frosted tips. Then again, who was she to judge? All she did was publish academic papers in obscure journals that most people didn't know about, let alone read. Even her students saw her as obsolete: a feminist dinosaur who hadn't caught up with the times, an old dyke with a big grudge against men. Tittering co-eds who thought that shaking their tits and grabbing their crotches on TV was hard evidence of the final liberation.

As if sex could be equated with freedom.

Darlene looked down at the computer perched on her lap and stared at the image on her screen saver. It was her favourite icon of the Madonna and child. The baby Jesus draped in white, face smiling, hand pointing the way to salvation, a miniature version of the adult prophet. And his mother, Mary, calm and serene, staring into space as if she was gazing into the future or contemplating some secret, hidden knowledge, her hand resting high on her belly as if she might be pregnant again.

Darlene hit the space bar and the image dissolved. Sex had been a kind of slavery for women, there was no denying that: slavery to children and motherhood, slavery to childbirth and death. But controlling sex hadn't brought the freedom they'd all expected, and that was the central irony. Sex could be fun, but it could also be dangerous, and it was far more complicated than her young students could ever imagine. Age and accident complicated it. Need and loyalty complicated it. But most of all, love and children complicated sex, and there was no use pretending that they didn't.

Her students were wrong about other things as well. Darlene didn't have a grudge against men per se, or even all men in general. Her father had been a fine human being and so had her husband, Ben, even though she hadn't managed to stay with him. Even though she had shattered him like a Christmas bauble on a concrete floor.

Darlene had always known that she was different, known since she was a child. But the full magnitude of the difference hadn't hit until she was twelve and went to see *The Truth about Spring*. Sitting in that dark theatre, watching Hayley Mills with her closely cropped blond hair and skin the milky-brown colour of a walnut shell, Darlene had fallen in love. How she had envied James MacArthur. How she had wanted to be him. And how she had wanted to be Hayley too, a tomboy called Spring who woke up one day in love, in the arms of a man. Darlene had wished so hard that eventually, she made it so. At the age of twenty-three, she met Ben and buried her schoolgirl fantasies about Spring so deep that she'd contemplated slitting her wrists to let them out again.

It had all been very melodramatic, of course. Her lying in the bathtub, razor poised, arm outstretched, having serious second thoughts as she stared at the single bead of blood forming along the tiniest pinprick of a cut. Ben arriving home unexpectedly and bursting through the bathroom door, saying that he needed to take a pee. He'd taken one look at her and fallen to his knees like someone had shot him in the leg.

He grabbed for a towel, wrapped it round her wrist and keened, "Why, Darlene? Why, Darlene?"

Darlene had just looked at him and whispered, "Because I'm in love with someone else."

And that was how it all began: with a lie and Darlene sitting stark naked in a bathtub, a full-sized towel wrapped around her arm like a cumbersome cast, with Ben sitting in the middle of the floor, sobbing as if his life had just come to an end. Darlene had gotten out of the tub, picked him up and led him to their bed, where they made love one last time. The next morning she got up, packed her things and left.

Two months later, Darlene discovered that she was pregnant. Two weeks after that, she had an abortion.

Now Darlene was too old to have a baby, and she didn't want to have a baby, but Athena did. And that's when all the trouble began: with Athena's longing for a child and the sudden reappearance of Spring.

Staring into the middle distance of memory, Darlene slowly registered the return of the perky little nurse. She stared at her laptop and tried to look busy, but it did no good. The little bubblehead just kept bouncing toward her.

"Hi, Ms Calder. Your mother's asleep, but you're

welcome to go in and sit with her now, if you like. I'm sure she'd love to see you when she wakes up. She's such a sweetie pie," the nurse said, pushing her lips together into a flat, smarmy little smile.

Darlene stared up into the vacant eyes of Nurse Happy Face. Were all these people mad? Were they confusing her mother with someone else?

"Look," she said, closing her computer with a snap. "I've been waiting to talk to her doctor for two hours. Is he still in her room?"

"No, I'm sorry, he's not. But he said he'd be back to speak with you as soon as he could."

"This is ridiculous," Darlene said, slamming her things together and shoving them into her briefcase. "I can't stay here all day. Is she all right or isn't she?"

"I'm sorry, *Miss* Calder," the nurse said, leaning on the "Miss" as if it were a veiled attack. "I can't tell you that. You'll have to wait until Dr. Weinman gets back."

Darlene gathered up the last of her things and snorted. It was so predictable. The perky ones always turned into self-righteous little bitches when they came up against someone who didn't buy their sweetness and light routine. She looked down at her hands and was surprised to see them shaking: strange how the brain could be thinking one thing while the body was feeling another.

Darlene picked up her briefcase and turned to face the doorway to her mother's room. What would she find there? What was she about to see?

She remembered the last days with her father. Thin and wasted and delirious from the morphine, he had drifted between this world and the next like a dried-out leaf buffeted by an arbitrary wind. In his lucid moments, he would make jokes and laugh. Then he'd suddenly look at her as if she wasn't there.

"They're coming to get us," he said, his eyes wide with terror.

"It's okay, Dad. You're in the hospital. No one's coming to get you."

"No, no. You can't see him, but I can. He's on the other side of that dike, and he's coming to get us."

"Who, Dad? Who's coming to get us?"

And just as suddenly as he'd left, her father came back. "Oh, Jesus," he said, his eyes glassy with tears. "I'm talking gibberish again, aren't I? It's these damn drugs. They turn your brains to pig shit."

"It's okay, Dad. Don't worry about it."

Then her father grinned as he always grinned when he wanted to push the world and her away. "You know, your mother always said I was crazy. Now I guess she's right," he said, reaching for the sponge stick that floated in the plastic cup of water on his bedside table.

Darlene got up, swished the sponge in the water and ran it across her father's lips. "Do you remember where you were, Dad?"

"Nowhere you'd want to be, Darlene. Nowhere on God's green earth anyone would want to be," her father said. Then he closed his eyes and slept.

Darlene pushed open the door to her mother's hospital room and peered in. The light was dim and a curtain was drawn around the bed closest to the window. In the bed nearest the door, a tiny, shriveled-up raisin of a woman turned over onto her back and started to snore, the low, rolling grunts gathering speed into a gale-force roar. Darlene made a mental note to add a private room to the list of requests in her living will, but as she turned away, the snoring stopped, and a thin voice hissed out from the raisin lady's bed.

"Get thee hence, Satan. Get thee hence, or I'll call down the Lord God Jesus on your head..."

Darlene turned to see the old lady sitting up, glaring at her, her right arm raised, index finger pointed, head cocked to the side like she was sighting down the barrel of a gun. Her face was flushed, and her hair stood straight up. Then just as abruptly as she'd sat up to greet Satan, the old lady fell back onto her pillows and seemed to fall asleep. Terrified that she'd just dropped dead, Darlene tiptoed over to the bed and leaned across the railing. The woman's eyes snapped open.

"You," the raisin lady rasped. "You are an abomination."

Darlene took a sharp step back, bumped into the table behind her and turned to watch as an empty plastic cup teetered on its side and fell, bouncing lightly across the floor. *Thank God it's not glass*, she thought, fumbling to catch it mid-bounce. Once she'd snagged it, she dropped it into the garbage pail next to the bed. When she looked up, the raisin lady's eyes were closed, her mouth was slack, and she was snoring again.

Darlene frowned. The old woman wasn't the first person in the world to call her a nasty name, and she likely wouldn't be the last. Still, it was a bit unnerving being mistaken for Satan in the hospital room where your mother might be drawing her last breath. Darlene thought about telling the story to Pearl. Maybe she'd change it a bit and say that the woman had called her Satan's spawn, daughter of Lady Lucifer lying in the next bed. Her mother would love that. Darlene could almost hear her laughing. She just hoped to God her mother could laugh.

Bracing herself for the shock, Darlene made her way to the curtain that encircled her mother's bed and drew it back. A great mound of a body lay perfectly still under a white sheet. At the top, she could just see her mother's face. Darlene couldn't remember ever seeing those features as calm as they were now. In sleep her mother looked younger somehow, the lines of her face smoothed out in rest. But the most surprising thing was the smile: the sad, serene, almost angelic smile that lit up her mother's face. It was so strange, so out of character, that Darlene just stood back and stared.

She had seen this smile before. Seen it on the face of Mary and the carved faces of the saints, and on Athena's face when she spoke of love and the coming of Spring.

Her name wasn't really Spring, of course. It was Georgia. She was one of Darlene's graduate students, a young woman from Great Britain who had breezed into Darlene's seminar room one day, with her blond hair and latte skin, and Darlene could hardly believe her eyes. There she was, Hayley Mills, her childhood fantasy, standing right there in front of her, and it was too late. Darlene was too old. She was too old for children, and she was certainly too old for Spring.

"You've got a crush on her, don't you?" Athena whispered in her ear at one of the graduate student parties.

"Don't be silly," Darlene said. "Georgia's twenty-three, and she's dating a football player. Even if I did have a crush on her, it wouldn't matter."

"I was twenty-six when you met me," she said. "And I was dating a man."

Sometimes Athena frightened the hell out of Darlene.

And it wasn't just the chakras and the crystals and the self-help books that scared her. It was Athena's insatiable need for love. That and her silent knowing, the look she'd get in her eyes, the gaze of the old soul, pixie smile of the wise. It was completely unnerving, like having a stranger see you naked or living with someone who could read your every thought.

And it was tiresome as well. Tiresome having someone love you so much, even when you were cranky and critical and remote. Sometimes Darlene just wanted to shake Athena and shout at her to fight back. But fighting back wasn't Athena's style. She was more at ease with watching and waiting. And that's what she would be doing when Darlene arrived home late, with her guilty conscience and her lame excuses.

She and Georgia had been doing their little courting ritual for months now: a coffee after class, a late afternoon visit to the office, dinner at the Pemmican Diner just off campus. Meetings filled with intense discussions about religion and the life of the spirit, about Mary and the goddesses of old. How in the early days, church fathers had built their cathedrals over the goddess temples and named them for Mary. How they had defanged vengeful Hera, desexualized Aphrodite and stripped Artemis of her bow and her female companions, and left in their place the quiet and serene, the all-suffering, all-knowing Mother, commanding that every woman on earth live up to her.

Small wonder Darlene was so ambivalent about her own mother. Pearl hadn't stood a chance.

And maybe that's what Georgia was really after – a divine mother who would support and mentor, love and protect, not some aging Sappho who lusted and yearned and wept for what was lost and what might still be. Darlene sighed as she sat down on the chair at the foot of the hospital bed and glanced up at the picture that hung on the wall above her mother's head. There she was, boy babe in arms, halo round her head, suffering on her lips, and beside her the sculpted image of her dead son, hanging on a shiny brass crucifix.

Sometimes Darlene wondered if she had been carrying a son. Other times, she was convinced that the speck in her uterus had been a girl. She knew that she wasn't supposed to have these thoughts. She was supposed to feel only relief. After all, she'd had no money. She had wanted to go back to school. What other choice had there been? But the grief was still there. It was always there, even though there was nothing she would have done differently.

Darlene got up and walked over to the table next to her mother's bed. The only things on it were a plastic water pitcher with an upside-down glass for a lid and her mother's beat-up leather purse. Darlene frowned as she remembered how adamant her mother had always been about the privacy of her handbag. "Don't go rummaging around in my purse. Just bring it to me if you want some money," she'd shout, convinced that when she sent her daughter to fetch her wallet, Darlene would use it as an excuse to rifle through her handbag, on the hunt for some secret or embarrassing thing.

On impulse, Darlene reached out and touched the worn gold clasp, snapped it open and peered inside. Nothing but a couple of used Kleenexes, a box of gum and a thin leather wallet. She picked up the wallet, opened it and saw a small scrap of paper folded between two five-dollar bills. She plucked it out and spread it open, expecting to find a grocery list. Instead she found a message, written in her father's hand, in soft grey pencil. "I love you," the note said, signed "You know who." Quietly and gently, Darlene re-folded the note and slid it back into Pearl's wallet. Then she turned and looked at her mother's face. The smile was all but gone, and her mother's lids were fluttering as if the eyes behind them were struggling to find something that had been lost. Darlene leaned back and closed her own eyes.

How many regrets did her mother have? How many regrets could one person live with before she simply gave up and died?

Darlene was never sure why she told her sister about the abortion. Maybe it was because Carol had been pregnant and married at seventeen. Perhaps because, at age twenty-four, her sister was raising two children on her own. Whatever the reason, the day Darlene scheduled her appointment she left the clinic, got on a bus and went straight to Carol's apartment to tell her what she'd done. With her two sons shrieking at the top of their lungs in the next room, her sister had seemed to barely register the news. Even when Darlene was finished, Carol just stared at her coffee cup.

"Are you sure about this?" she finally asked.

Darlene nodded, resting her hand on her own cup, rubbing its rough, chipped edge against the soft flesh of her thumb, listening to the laughter of the children in the next room, waiting for Carol to say something, waiting for some sign of reassurance. When none came, she finally asked what she feared her sister was thinking.

"Am I doing the wrong thing?"

Before she could answer, Carol's three-year-old son ran

screaming into the kitchen. His older brother had just clubbed him over the head with a Tonka truck, and he was bleeding from a small cut on his forehead. Carol picked him up, dabbed at the blood with a Kleenex then turned to face Darlene. She looked like someone who was drowning, like someone who could never be saved.

"I don't know, Darlene," she said, shifting her son's weight onto her hip and walking into the living room to deal with his older brother.

"Professor Calder?" a man's voice asked.

"Yes," Darlene said, turning to look up into the eyes of a man dressed, like the walls, in hospital green.

"I'm Dr. Weinman," he said and knelt down next to her chair. "How's she doing?"

"I don't know. She's still asleep. Is she going to be all right?"

"I think so, yes. She had a minor stroke, but she should be fine. We'll just keep her in for a couple of days to monitor things."

"Can she talk? Is she paralyzed?"

"No, no, she's fine. She might be a little muddled when she wakes up, but she should get back to normal. We've adjusted her blood pressure medication and given her something to deal with the clot. And we'll keep her here for a few days just to be sure. Episodes like this can sometimes be followed by something more serious, so we have to monitor for that."

"More serious? What do you mean?"

"A possible heart attack or another stoke," he said and got to his feet. "But don't worry, I'm sure she'll be fine. I'll be back in an hour or so to check her over when she wakes up."

When Dr. Weinman got as far as the curtain, he stopped, turned back and smiled at Darlene. "And by the way," he said. "When will your father be coming in? She seemed pretty anxious to see him."

Darlene stared at him in bewilderment. "My father's dead. He died six months ago."

"Oh," he said. "I'm sorry about that. Well, she'll likely remember when she wakes up. The memory loss is usually temporary."

When he was gone, Darlene got up, walked over to the edge of the bed and looked down at her mother's face. So perhaps that was it. Perhaps the source of her mother's smile was not wisdom but forgetting: the smile of a woman with no regrets, just the sweet delight of the now.

Darlene closed her eyes and gripped the metal guardrail at the side of her mother's bed. What in God's name was she doing? All those years of self-righteous distain aimed at her male colleagues and their dalliances with twenty-year-old students, and now here she was, a fifty-year-old cliché poised to do the same thing. Drowning in guilt but loving the thrill – the secret trysts, the furtive phone calls. She had called Georgia that morning, and her hello had been thick and gravelly and sexy with sleep.

"Oh God, I'm sorry, Georgia. Did I wake you up?"

"No, no, it's fine. I'm awake. What's up?"

"I'm sorry about this, but I have to cancel lunch today."

"Oh," Georgia said, her voice suddenly alert. "Is something wrong?"

"Sort of. Yes. My mother was just taken to the hospital."

"Oh no. Is she all right? What happened?"

"I don't know. Her friend Jean was there, but she was crying so hard I could barely understand what she was saying. But, Georgia, look, I've got to go. My ride'll be here any minute, and I'm supposed to be waiting outside."

Darlene winced as the words slipped out of her mouth. *My ride.* That was who Athena had become: someone nameless, a cab driver, an old friend giving her a lift.

"Hold on. Professor Calder? What hospital is your mother in?"

Oh God, why was she asking that? And why had she lapsed back into calling her Professor Calder? The combination of formal address and intimate demand left Darlene speechless. Did Georgia actually expect to come to the hospital? Surely not.

"Are you still there?" Georgia asked.

"Yes, yes, I'm here. She's at the Hotel Dieu, but, Georgia, listen. I'll call you later. Let you know what's happening."

Now it was Georgia's turn to fall silent. When she spoke again, her voice was tight and clipped. "Sure. I'll talk to you then, I guess," she said, and hung up before Darlene could say goodbye.

Darlene stared at her cell phone then clicked it off and hurried out the front door to the car that was waiting outside. Was Georgia really that young, that insensitive? When she looked up, she saw Athena waiting by the car, her face full of sympathy, her arms reaching out in comfort. Instead of welcoming the embrace, Darlene raised her hands.

"I can't go there, Thena. If I do, I'll just start to cry."

"Maybe crying would help," Athena said, but before Darlene could answer, she turned away and walked around to the driver's side.

Was it hurt or pity Darlene had seen in her eyes? She could never be quite sure. She got into the car and studied the windshield. "You know what I'm like. Can't you just leave it alone?"

They drove the rest of the way in silence until Athena pulled up at the emergency room entrance. "Do you want me to come in with you?"

"No, there's no point. I'll just be waiting around. You should go back to work. If I need anything, I'll call."

"Is there anything I can do for you?"

"You can call Carol. I haven't been able to reach her."

"Okay. When I know she's on her way to the hospital, I'll come and pick you up."

"You'll just wind up waiting, Athena," Darlene said, unable to keep the irritation out of her voice.

"I don't mind waiting," Athena said quietly. "You know that."

Darlene yanked on the door handle and got out of the car. By the time she turned around, Athena was waiting for her on the driver's side.

"You need to forgive her, Darlene," she said.

Here it comes. Not this. Not now.

"Forgive her for what, Athena?" Darlene snapped. "Exactly what is it that I'm supposed to forgive my mother for?"

When Athena finally spoke, she didn't shout or plead. She just spoke quietly, as if resigned to her fate. "I don't know, Darlene, but you'd better figure it out, because I'm getting pretty tired of this," she said and turned toward the car. "Give your mother my love. Tell her I hope she gets well. Tell her I'll be thinking of her."

Darlene wanted to call her back, say she was sorry, but instead she just stood there while Athena drove away. She watched the car until it disappeared.

Now she stared down at her mother. She had never allowed herself to imagine this: that her mother might die, that Athena might be the one to leave her.

Darlene sat down on the chair next to her mother's bed. Pearl's left hand rested on her thigh, the thin gold band on her ring finger cutting into her flesh. What did Darlene really know about this woman? She'd always assumed that her mother had never really loved her father. Now she wasn't so sure. All she really had was the story, the one she told to make sense of her own life: the myth of the loud, impatient woman, the one who didn't like to be touched, the one who didn't cry.

"Now don't go getting all mushy on me." Her mother had bristled when Darlene reached out to embrace her after her father's funeral. "I've got too many things on my mind."

At the time, Darlene had reacted as if she'd been slapped. Now she found herself wondering, wondering about all the things that might have been swirling around in her mother's head, all the people and the memories Darlene knew nothing about, because she had never asked. She never asked because she'd always been too busy keeping her own secrets, telling her own lies.

"What in God's name is wrong with you?" her mother had asked when she'd walked in the door of Darlene's bachelor apartment and found her dressed in her pajamas, her eyes red from crying.

"Nothing's wrong," Darlene said, blowing her nose and lying back down on the pullout couch. "It's just my period. Just a really shitty day."

"Then get up and start moving around," her mother ordered as she stomped to the closet and hauled out the vacuum. "This place is a goddamned pigsty."

Darlene turned her face to the wall, willing her mother to stop talking, willing her to leave, hoping against hope that Pearl couldn't see the rush of blood that was leaking through her pad and into the crotch of her flannel pajamas. But her mother just kept on talking about dusters and cleaning fluids, about toilet brushes and Mr. Clean. Then she suddenly stopped talking, and Darlene felt the heavy weight of her mother's body on the other side of the bed.

"Is it Ben, Darlene? Is that what's got you so upset? Are you having second thoughts about the separation?"

It had never occurred to Darlene to tell her mother the truth. She had just turned over and lied. Lied about asking Ben to have her back. Lied about his rejection. Lied about the abortion and her life. And in her heart she blamed her mother for the lies. Blamed her for being the kind of woman who couldn't handle the truth, for being someone who would never understand. But it wasn't her mother who had avoided the truth, and it wasn't her mother who had lied.

"What's done is done, Darlene. There's no sense crying over spilt milk. It doesn't change what is," had been her mother's harsh reply.

What Darlene had forgotten to remember was that her mother had spoken softly and reached out as if to touch her hand.

Darlene turned away from the hospital window and reached out to rest her own hand on her mother's arm. As she did, Pearl's eyes opened.

"My sweet girl," she said, then turned over and closed her eyes.

CHAPTER 6

2000

There were days when she felt that she had the most meaningful job in the world. Helping women to feel better, particularly older women, filled her with a sense of pride and purpose. But there was one woman who might undo all that, one old lady who might defeat even the skill of a cosmetological goddess like Athena. That woman was Mrs. Tuttle, and Mrs. Tuttle had the feet of a tortoise: the kind of feet that every esthetician dreads: feet that were the stuff of nightmares.

Athena had tried everything – soapy footbaths and hot paraffin, pumice stone and cream – and still Mrs. Tuttle's feet remained unchanged. The calluses didn't budge, the great horny toenails persisted, hard as stone, and the quarter-inch heel leather held fast, undiminished. To make matters worse, Mrs. Tuttle's feet were always swollen: the shank of each foot like a roll of pre-risen bread dough, each toe like a fat Italian sausage sticking out the end. They reminded her of the snack Darlene's mother made:

pigs in a blanket. Athena couldn't eat the sausage rolls because of Mrs. Tuttle's feet. Darlene was aghast when Athena told the story to Pearl, but Pearl had laughed so hard she'd slopped coffee onto her chest.

Athena could never understand why Darlene was so aloof with her mother, so angry and ungenerous. It was true that Pearl was blunt and irritable, but it was also true that she loved her daughter. She loved her the best way she could. But even more remarkable, Pearl had accepted them as a couple, and for that alone, Athena would always be grateful. She just hoped Pearl would survive long enough to make peace with Darlene, because if Darlene made peace with her mother then there was hope that she would accept what Athena had done.

Athena said a silent prayer for Pearl then sat down at her station and got back to work. She visualized Mrs. Tuttle's feet and scanned her arsenal. There was the collagen foot cream she'd tried at the last appointment, and the Foot So Soft treatment she'd tried two weeks before. She might consider using the heel razor, but that always made her nervous. Athena didn't like using blades or machines in her work. They just made her clients sore and uncomfortable, and what was the point of that? Women came to the spa to relax and escape the pain in their lives, not replace it with another kind of pain. They wanted to be touched and stroked, they wanted to feel pampered and beautiful, and how could you feel that with a silly machine buzzing in your ear? Besides, a calm face was always a beautiful face, no matter how deep the crow's feet or the laugh lines.

Athena reached across the desk, turned on the disc player, and Bach's "Cello Suite in D Minor" bathed the room in blue. Swelling with sorrow and longing, radiant in joyful belief, Bach's music was always blue; it was indigo and azure, cobalt and sky. Athena knew the colour of his music because she saw it, just as she saw the auras that illuminated the people around her. Her lover's aura was yellow, sometimes pure as sunlight, other times the colour of clay. Lately, flashes of red appeared in Darlene's aura, especially when Athena spoke of wanting a child.

Athena lifted her mortar and pestle from the shelf above her head, poured oil into the marble bowl, added a handful of scented crystals and began to grind, hoping that the new mixture would soften Mrs. Tuttle's armoured feet. Poor Mrs. Tuttle had a grey, pea-green aura. Grey was not a good colour for people, and this particular grey-green was deadly, like the colour of things that had been closed up and shut away, things that couldn't breathe, grew mould and went to rot.

There was no doubt in Athena's mind that people could wind up covered in mould, even if they didn't see it that way. Every skin and nail affliction in the world could be seen as evidence of something spoiling in a person's heart. She'd seen many women in just that condition. Mothers who did nothing but chase children and beg their husbands for help, grandmothers who had never traveled further than a hundred miles from their own homes, businesswomen so closed up and clenched down that their faces became a road map of every psychic kick in the ass they'd ever received. Athena believed that it was her mission to destroy the mould and vanquish the pain so that all of her clients could feel well and whole again, if only for a little while.

But for poor Mrs. Tuttle, it might be too late.

It had been too late for Athena's mother as well. Two days after Athena graduated from the Touch of Paris

School for Estheticians, her mother had taken a swan dive off the Otter Street Bridge and landed in the muddy waters of the Assiniboine. According to the policeman who had tried to talk her down, her mother hadn't been trying to kill herself. She'd simply been convinced that she could fly. They found her body caught on a sand bar, surrounded by sunken beer bottles tossed into the water by teenagers – teenagers who might have learned to play "Für Elise" in the living room of her mother's apartment.

Athena closed her eyes, trying to shut out the images of that day. Her mother's face bloated by pills and river water, her hands resting on a white sheet, the nails broken and blue, but the fingers still long and shapely: a musician's hands.

Athena opened her eyes and stared into the cold grey-white of the marble vessel, remembering how her mother's music had filled their house with such sorrow and joy. How her mother's skin was soft and warm and smelled of patchouli and powder. How every Friday night, when Athena was very small, her mother would do up her hair and dress in something long and flowing. How she would fill the tables with food and wine, light the rooms with candles and shut the drapes as violinists and cellists, oboe players and flautists gathered in the house to play. The soft, yellow light glinting from the music stands, the air filled with candle smoke, the musky scent of gardenias, sweet-cherry pipe tobacco and the colours of the music – colours that drifted up the stairs, easing Athena into the sweetest of dreams.

Athena's father, who could not tell one note from another, had loved those evenings. Athena had seen it for herself. Crouched on the stairs, she had watched her father watching her mother, his eyes like those of a thirsty man, drinking her in. But in the end, Athena's mother had proved to be too much for him, too much in every way.

"Don't go, Colin. I couldn't bear it."

"Then stop lying to me, Lilly. Stop the craziness, and I'll stay."

Bach's "Air on a G String" filled the room, the cello's first long note and vibrato conjuring images of women gliding down hallways or standing, gazing out of windows, waiting just as her mother had waited.

Athena rested her hand on her belly. What would Darlene say, she wondered? How would she react? Athena closed her eyes, but all she could see was crimson bleeding through dark ochre-yellow.

"Mrs. Tuttle is here, Athena."

Athena opened her eyes to find the squat, compact body of her business partner, Cindy, standing in the doorway. "I'll be there in a few minutes," she said, reaching over to turn the music down.

"No," Cindy said, folding her arms across her chest. "You'd better come now. She's in a bit of a state."

"What's the problem?"

"I don't know, but she's sitting there crying, and my next client looks like she's ready to bolt. If she sits there much longer, Mrs. Tuttle's going to scare her off."

Athena followed Cindy down the hallway and found Mrs. Tuttle staring at the waiting room wall, clutching a soggy tissue. Athena sat down beside her and reached out to take her hand, but Mrs. Tuttle shook her head.

"I don't know what's wrong with me," she said between little gasping breaths. "Every time I walk in here, I start to cry."

"That's perfectly understandable," Athena said, putting her hand under Mrs. Tuttle's elbow and helping her up.

"Your feet are coming alive again. It can be very painful when that happens."

"Good Lord," Mrs. Tuttle said, shaking off Athena's hand and tucking her elbows in under her ribcage to straighten herself up. "You do say the strangest things. They're just feet, you know. And they don't feel much one way or the other. Just pain. That's all my feet feel."

Athena did her best to keep smiling as she steered Mrs. Tuttle into the pedicure room. Women like this were almost as bad as the men they married. Crying just wasn't done. So when they finally did let loose, it terrified them, because it felt as if it might never end.

"Now, you just sit right there, Mrs. Tuttle, while I prepare your foot bath."

"I wore my nylon knee highs this time," Mrs. Tuttle said with a grunt as she reached down to roll up the leg of her navy blue stretch pants. "I hate the stupid things, but it's better than panty hose. I hate having to take everything off just to get at my feet."

Athena stared at the nylon-encased sausage rolls and frowned. "It might be better if you wore something that breathes. Like cotton socks?"

"Good heavens," Mrs. Tuttle said, tucking her chin into her neck and furrowing her brow. "I haven't worn socks since I was a girl."

"Well, it was just a thought." Athena turned back to the counter to get the mixture of oil and crystals for the foot bath. "Have you been soaking your feet in Epsom salts like I suggested?"

"No, no. I can't be bothered with all that nonsense," Mrs. Tuttle said. She stretched an elongated tube of puce-coloured nylon off her toes with a snap and presented her foot to Athena. "But my friend Edith suggested I soak them in dish detergent and bleach. They look a bit better, don't you think?"

Athena stared at the huge, gnarled toenails, and her heart sank. "Well, they do look a bit better, don't they?" Athena averted her eyes, turned on the water in the foot sink and poured in her newest softening concoction.

"Not too hot, now. I don't like it too hot," Mrs. Tuttle said, her lower lip quivering, her eyes fogging up with tears as she stared at the bubbles forming in the water.

Athena patted her knee. " Don't you worry, I know just how you like it. Now put your feet in there to soak, and I'll be back in ten minutes with your tea." Athena got up, turned the dial on the timer and walked toward the door.

"Well, don't put any milk in it this time. I hate milk. I take my tea black...and not too strong," Mrs. Tuttle called out after her. "It gets me all worked up if it's too strong,"

Athena walked into the hallway, stopped and pressed her hand against the wall. Mrs. Tuttle made her feel dizzy, as dizzy as she had sometimes felt as a child.

The doctors called it manic depression and gave her mother pills, but her mother hated them and kept flushing them down the toilet. The lithium lassitude, she called it, the day and night of the living dead.

"White pills, grey life, Thena. All the colours seep away and I can't play. But your father isn't too happy, so he's leaving us for a while," her mother said.

When she was seven, her father left and never came back, and Athena stayed with her mother – the incandescent Mary Poppins one day, violin in one hand, bow in the other, soaring over the mundane on an updraft of wild enthusiasm, and sad Ophelia the next, clutching an empty gin bottle and staring into space, her body pinned to the ground, her spirit drifting in a dark and silent place. Even after her mother finally agreed to take the pills and grew huge and bloated with lithium and food, some part of her true spirit remained like the aura that lingers behind a fragment of music you hear and forget and long to remember.

The kettle whistled, and Athena pulled it off the ring, dropped a single tea bag into the pot and left it on the countertop to steep. She closed her eyes, took a deep breath, locked her throat and sent her breath upwards, into the seventh chakra. The Jalandhara Bandha always filled her with energy and calmed her mind. When she finished, she closed her eyes again, cradled her hand under her belly and took another breath. This time she sent it deep into the nether regions of her body, puffing it out in short, steady breaths. When she was done, she stood very still, listening for the heartbeat, feeling the life force of oxygen rushing through her body and into the body of her child.

Athena was ten weeks and two days pregnant: almost past the danger period, finally at the point where she could no longer hide the pregnancy from Darlene. She knew it was wrong to have hidden it from her, to have gone ahead and done it without Darlene's involvement or consent. But time was running out. Athena was thirty-eight, and she couldn't be sure that Darlene would ever want a child.

"I'm almost fifty," Darlene said. "I'm too old for kids. Too set in my ways."

Athena leaned against the counter. What did people mean when they said things like that? It made it sound as if Darlene were fixed in concrete, and nothing could be further from the truth. If that were true, then Darlene wouldn't be toying with the idea of having an affair with a woman half her age.

"I'm selfish," she said. "I like my freedom."

Athena poured herself a cup of tea. It wasn't as if she'd done it to trap Darlene. She wasn't that kind of woman. But she hadn't really thought it through either, hadn't faced what it would mean to raise a child alone. She'd just booked the appointments. Two weeks after the second insemination, she discovered she was pregnant. She had been ecstatic when she went to see the doctor. The only sadness came when she realized she had no one to share it with.

So she had decided, then and there, not to keep it a secret any longer. She left the doctor's office and drove straight to the university to tell Darlene what she had done, imagining along the way every possible scenario but the one that had actually occurred. Just as she turned the corner that led to the long, narrow hallway outside Darlene's office, one of her graduate students, the girl with the short blond hair, had walked out of the office door, with Darlene following close behind. Both of them were laughing, their voices bouncing down the narrow space. Athena had stepped back just as the girl grabbed Darlene's hand and began pulling her down the hallway in the opposite direction.

"Come on," she heard the girl say. "Forget about work. Let's just go."

For a split second it seemed as if Darlene might resist, but in the end she followed the girl.

Athena knew that she should have stopped them. She should have called out and announced her presence. Instead she just ran for her car, driving it to the parking lot and waiting near the exit, until Darlene and the girl finally appeared. It had all been so humiliating. Her ducking down to avoid being seen, Darlene driving out of the lot and onto the crescent, with Athena following along behind.

She had expected them to turn off into one of the small motel lots that lined the strip. Instead, they pulled in at a restaurant, and Athena kept driving, down the highway and out of the city, where she finally turned off into an empty field.

It was early April and the snow was all but gone. Athena got out of her car, pulled her coat tight against the cold spring wind and waited while the sun sank toward the horizon. What if her imaginings were wrong? What if it was nothing more than an innocent friendship between a teacher and her student? Or worse. What if Darlene simply didn't want to raise a child with her?

"I don't think I'd be a very good mother, do you? You're the one who's always telling me how impatient I am. What if the kid takes after me?" Darlene had asked.

But maybe that wasn't really what Darlene was worried about.

Standing in the spa kitchen, Athena closed her eyes, cleared her mind of memory and drew in another deep breath.

"What will be will be," she said.

It was the mantra she always used whenever she contemplated confronting Darlene or telling her what she had done, the only words that calmed her down when she thought about raising her daughter alone. Athena knew that staying calm was essential for the baby, so she drew in the Mula Bandha, the breath of life, and sent it into her belly from deep inside her chest.

If Mrs. Tuttle had been more open, Athena would have taught her the Mula Bandha, the way to direct her breath into the root chakra, centre for the legs and feet, source of her pain and instability. But if Athena had tried to explain the Mula Bandha to Mrs. Tuttle, the old woman would have thought she'd lost her mind, so there wasn't much point.

The timer went off. Athena poured a cup of tea for Mrs. Tuttle and headed back down the hall to the pedicure room. She felt more herself now: calm, almost ethereal. The spa's frosty grey walls soothed her, and the Frida Kahlo portrait that hung on the wall opposite her pedicure room called out to her to stop and look.

Beautiful, sad Frida, dressed in vibrant red and yellow, her back to a fecund and encroaching jungle, a parrot perched on her shoulder, her eyes like those of a tigress and a deer. Eyes that had given birth to paintings, a body that could never bear the child she so desperately wanted.

Whose eyes would Athena's daughter have? Would they be hers, or would they be her mother's? And if they were her mother's, what would that mean?

Athena turned and opened the door to the pedicure room. When she spotted Mrs. Tuttle, she almost dropped her teacup. The old woman lay sprawled back on the chair, her mouth open, her breathing shallow, and there wasn't a speck of colour illuminating her head.

"Mrs. Tuttle? Mrs. Tuttle, are you all right?"

Mrs. Tuttle's eyes flew open, her mouth slammed shut and a bright red light shot straight up from the crown of her head. She clutched her chest.

"Good Lord," she said, the grey-green cloud of her aura pulsing into life again. "You shouldn't sneak up on people like that. I could have had a heart attack."

"I'm sorry, Mrs. Tuttle," Athena said, sucking back a sigh of relief. "How do your feet look?"

"Like boiled lobsters," Mrs. Tuttle said flatly as she

lifted one foot then the other out of the bubbling water of the footbath.

Athena squeezed some cream into her palm, sat down on a stool and lifted Mrs. Tuttle's right foot onto her lap. She stroked the hard, red skin, ran her fingertips under the scaly heel and was surprised to feel it give a little to her touch. Even the claws seemed softer.

"I think we've made a breakthrough. Do they feel any better?"

"No," Mrs. Tuttle said, a little tear squeezing out the side of her right eye. "And for pity's sakes, go easy. Don't press so hard. You don't know your own strength. Just look at those hands of yours. They're huge. Where in God's name did you get hands like that?"

Athena spread her hands in front of her like a pair of fleshy wings and stared at them.

"Wake up, Thena. Wake up, honey. It's time to play."

"No, Mommy, please. I want to sleep."

"Come on, Thena. It's too beautiful to sleep. The moon is out and the stars are shining and it's time to play. We have to play, Thena, or the moon will go away."

"I'm so tired, Mommy," Athena said, but when she lifted her head from the pillow and peered into the darkness, she found she was talking to thin air. Her mother had already disappeared.

Athena swung her legs out and dangled her feet over the side of the bed, her toes brushing the smooth, icy surface of the linoleum. What should she do? How would she ever get up for school in the morning? And if she did go, who would look after her mother? Maybe she could ask one of the old ladies who lived on their floor, but that would mean telling them that her mother was sick, and she didn't think that would be a good idea. Her mother didn't look sick. Sometimes, she didn't even sound sick. They might think she was lying. Then, if there were a real emergency, no one would come, and Athena would be alone. No, she'd be better off waiting and asking for help when she really needed it. Her mother would be all right. This had happened before. Athena would be late for school. Maybe she wouldn't even go to school. But her mother would be all right.

Stepping down onto her tiptoes, Athena scanned the darkness for her slippers, spotted them near the closet door and hesitated. She didn't want to go near the closet. There might be something in there – something hanging on the inside hook or scrabbling around under the shoe board – so she padded slowly and silently around the edges of the room, and when she got close enough she darted out the door. By the time she reached the hallway, her feet were so cold that her shins ached, but there was a warm light coming from the living room, so she ran towards it. When she got there, she found candles glowing everywhere, perched on every surface of the room, the wax dripping onto the backs of the armchairs, oozing across the surface of the piano, sliding down the glass eye of the TV.

The magic and beauty of it all overwhelmed her fear, and she smiled.

"Isn't it wonderful?" her mother said, holding her arms up and twirling around and around in the centre of the room. "I brought the stars inside. Now go and get your cello, darling, and we'll play to the moon."

Athena walked to the couch and pulled the cello out from behind it. She opened the case, slid the bow out from

under its clip, lifted out the half-size cello and dragged it
to one of the kitchen chairs her mother had set in front of
the living room window. She sat down, pulled her flannel
nightgown up over her bony knees, spread her legs and
leaned the icy neck of the cello against her shoulder. Then
she looked up through the open window. The man in the
moon was huge, full, glowing pink, his eyes wide open
above a cavernous grin.

"You see," her mother said as she knelt beside her and
pointed up at the window, her eyes lit up with a transcen-
dent glow, the muscles in her face tightening in the mania
of a hopeless belief. "The moon is smiling down on us, and
if we play just right, your father will come home, and every
day will be wonderful. As wonderful as this very night."

When she finished, her mother took her seat, picked up
her violin and lifted the bow with her right hand, the long,
elegant fingers of her left poised over the strings. Athena
laid her head against the smooth, hard wood of the cello,
but nothing happened. No music came. She got up, laid
the cello on the floor, walked over to her mother and held
out her hand.

"They're just like mine, Thena," her mother said, cup-
ping the small hand with her own, her tears dropping and
pooling in the tiny palm as she brushed her lips across the
tips of Athena's fingers. "They're just like mine."

Athena looked at Mrs. Tuttle's face. Her eyes were closed
and her face seemed to register nothing: not pleasure, not
unhappiness, not even pain.

Sometimes Athena wondered if her mother had been
crazy at all. Maybe she had just seen things and felt things
to which other human beings were immune: as if she had

no skin, no barrier, no way to filter out the beautiful, baleful onslaught of the world. Sometimes Athena felt that she was like her mother: that she too saw the great magic of life's light, its colour and music. But in her heart, Athena knew that she was not her mother. Her mother had been mentally ill, and she was sane – sane enough to know that a life lived with no magic was really no life at all.

Athena lifted Mrs. Tuttle's foot from her lap and rested it on the floor.

"Oh dear," Mrs. Tuttle said, looking down at her feet like a child staring at a birthday gift she didn't want and hadn't asked for. "Is it over already? Couldn't you just keep going a little longer?"

Athena shook her head. "I'm sorry, Mrs. Tuttle. I have another client coming in five minutes."

"Then I suppose this will have to do," Mrs. Tuttle snapped, snatching her nylon knee-highs from the chair beside her.

"Should I book you for the same time next week? "

"Oh, I suppose so, but I don't know why I bother. I've been coming here for months now, and I still don't see much improvement. And these sessions are costing me a fortune."

"I could recommend someone else. There are lots of good people in town."

"Oh, never mind that. You're not pawning me off on someone else now. It's too late for that," Mrs. Tuttle said, stomping toward the door like a great bowlegged turtle, dragging her misery behind her like a huge grey shell.

"I can't stand it any more," her mother had said. "I'd rather die."

Athena bent over, pulled the plug in the foot sink and got the cleaning spray out of the cupboard. And as she scrubbed away the hard grey residue of Mrs. Tuttle's feet, she decided that she would go home and tell Darlene that she was pregnant. If Darlene left, that would be her choice. Athena would manage just as her mother had managed. Maybe better, certainly no worse.

CHAPTER 7

2000

Carol could feel the breeze Darlene's arms blew up as she waved her hands around like a couple of flyswatters, trying to beat back a cloud of mosquitoes. She yanked on the door again and wiggled the key, but the lock wouldn't budge.

"Are you sure you've got the right one?" Darlene asked, the sound of her frustration bouncing up and down in time to the motion of her flailing arms.

"I'm not stupid, Darlene. Of course I've got the right key. She gave it to me."

As she spoke, the tumblers finally gave, the key slid around in the lock, and Darlene crowded in behind her as she pushed open the door. Carol took two steps inside, and the shock of what she saw stopped her in her tracks. Darlene groaned as she stumbled into Carol's back.

"Jesus, Carol, move. The mosquitoes are killing me."

"I can't move," Carol said, taking three short steps forward. She stopped again, blocked this time by a card table laden down with kitchenware: rows of mismatched cups and glasses, an old egg beater, a pastry blender with a red handle, most of the paint worn away by years of apple pies. The living room was just as her mother's friend Izzie had described it. Every surface, every square inch of floor space was crammed with garage sale items.

"Jean got a couple of the neighbours to give her a hand," Izzie had said, "while I rode in the ambulance with your mother. She said it was a real mess in there, but she didn't know what to do with it all, and she wanted to get up to the hospital as fast as she could."

Carol held on to the edge of the table, while Darlene stepped over a box of Tupperware and inspected the room.

"Christ," she said, picking up an old extension cord and tossing it back onto the floor. "What the hell are we supposed to do with all this stuff? It'll take forever to sort it out. I don't know what she wants to keep."

Carol stared down at a pile of her father's clothing. The sight of it made her want to weep, until she looked up and spotted the food processor, sitting on top of a TV table. She climbed over a cardboard box, peered at the price tag and gasped. "That thing cost me a hundred and fifty dollars," she said, pointing at the food processor. "And she was going to sell it for a dollar fifty."

"Well, at least she didn't throw it out." Darlene laughed, but as she zigzagged her way through a pile of books, the laughter faded. "I don't believe this," she said, staring at something on the floor. She bent down and picked up a tin dollhouse with a red roof and a painted vine climbing up the wall. "She was going to sell my dollhouse."

Carol folded her arms. "Oh, fine. She can sell my gift, but heaven forbid she sell your precious dollhouse?"

"This is different, Carol. This is about my childhood."

"It's always different when it's about you," Carol said. She swung her body around, bent on making a dramatic exit, only to discover that she was hemmed in by a sea of boxes.

By the time she turned around again, Darlene was sitting in the only available space on the couch, staring at a tower of paperbacks stacked on the coffee table.

"What in God's name was she doing? It's like she was trying to wipe out her entire life."

Carol reached down and picked up the small china spaniel that sat on the end table next to her. She fingered its smooth, glossy body and peeled off the ten-cent sticker her mother had stuck to its belly.

"She wasn't just wiping out *her* life," Carol said and slipped the china spaniel into her pocket.

They were more careful with one another after that. They didn't argue. In fact, when Darlene held up their mother's Blue Mountain pottery poodle, they both laughed.

"Remember this?" she said.

How could Carol forget?

They'd been playing school in the living room, and as usual, Darlene had been the teacher, Carol the student. When Darlene refused to reverse their roles, they got into a tussle, and before they knew it, the long-necked Blue Mountain pottery poodle had tipped over. Its body lay on the coffee table, its head on the floor, decapitated by the sharp edge of Arborite.

Terrified, she and Darlene had picked up the pieces and raced down the basement stairs to find the glue. After an hour of fiddling, they finally managed to stick the dog's turquoise and black head back onto its body.

"She'll never notice," Darlene assured her.

But Carol knew that she and her sister could never put anything past their mother. They were playing cutouts upstairs when they heard her bellow from below. "Carol! Darlene! Get down here now."

"Which one of you did this?" she asked, pointing at the poodle.

It was only then that both girls realized that they had glued the dog's head on backward. They stood there as their mother ranted and raved at them, accusing them of not valuing her things. Then she sent them to bed without any supper.

At eight o'clock that night, they were in bed reading comics when their father snuck up the stairs with two peanut butter and honey sandwiches and a glass of milk to share.

"Don't tell your mother," he said. "And don't worry. I'll fix it."

Carol folded the last of her father's sweaters and put them into the green garbage bag in front of her. Why hadn't her mother dealt with his things sooner? It had been almost six months since he died. That was ample time to dispose of his belongings. And why had she decided to sell his clothes rather than give them away or donate them to some charitable organization, like the Kidney Foundation or Camps for Kids?

Carol pulled on the neck of the bag and screwed it together with a long twist tie. Because her mother was a hard-hearted bitch, that's why. Because only a hard-hearted bitch would sell her husband's things after he died.

She was about to drag the bag to the other side of the

room when she noticed Darlene staring at it as if she wanted to rip it open to see what was inside. Darlene had been doing this all morning, questioning the contents of every box and bag she put in the donate pile as if she didn't trust Carol's ability to make a decision about anything.

"It's Dad's clothes, Darlene."

"Oh, sorry. I was just curious."

Carol dumped the bag onto the growing pile, strode back to her side of the room and slid another cardboard box into the empty space in front of her.

"Do you want to keep this, or should I throw it out?" Darlene was holding up a small zippered sweater, powder blue with a white kitten on each of the side panels and two kittens playing with a ball of pink yarn on the back. Carol smiled in spite of herself. Her mother had knit that sweater as a Christmas gift, and when Carol opened it, she'd forgotten all about the Betsy-Wetsy doll Santa Claus had given her.

How many hours had her mother spent knitting that sweater, late at night, long after she and Darlene had gone to bed? How had she known that Carol's favourite colour was blue or that she secretly and desperately wanted a cat?

Carol frowned. This was the way it always went. This was her life: one long series of mixed messages from her mother.

"I think you should keep it," Darlene said, scrutinizing the sweater. "It still looks good. Maybe someone else could use it."

"Whatever," Carol said, pulling on the flaps of another cardboard box. She stopped what she was doing and pointed at the couch. "Just toss it on the pile."

She turned back to the box, yanked it open and found herself staring into dozens of glass eyes. There had to be more than twenty dolls nestled inside the cardboard, dolls of all shapes and sizes: Barbies and Barbie wannabes, walking dolls, bride dolls and babies.

Carol had always dreamt of giving her old dolls to her daughter, but Nathan had been content with the two boys. "I'm happy to raise your kids, but I don't want kids of my own."

Carol had been so relieved to find a new husband and a safe home for her sons that she had accepted Nathan's terms, despite the fact that she had always wanted a daughter, a little girl to whom she could have given all of the things she had and had never had.

But it was too late for that now, so Carol closed the flaps on the box and carried it to the other side of the room.

"What's in there?" Darlene asked, pointing at the box.

Carol finally snapped. "For God's sake, Darlene. I'm not giving away anything important. It's just a bunch of old dolls."

"Well, hold on a minute," Darlene said, hurrying across the room. She bent over and started digging through the box. "I might want to keep a few."

Carol threw up her hands. "What for? You don't have kids."

Darlene straightened up. She had a baby doll in one hand and a Barbie in the other. She tossed them both back into the box.

"Athena's pregnant," she said.

"What?" Carol gasped. "She had an affair?"

"No, I was about to do that. She just went and got herself inseminated."

Carol set a coffee cup on the kitchen table in front of her sister and went back to preparing lunch. "Has she had an ultrasound yet?"

Darlene nodded and stared out the window. "I still can't believe she did this. I told her I didn't want kids and she goes ahead and does it anyway, without even telling me. Then she waltzes in and just blurts it out: 'I'm eleven weeks pregnant,' she says. How the hell did she think I was going to react?"

"Well, how did you react?"

"How do you think? I was furious. I'd never have done something like that to her."

"Oh, for God's sake, Darlene."

Darlene's head slumped into her hands. "It's not an affair, Carol. We're not having sex. I told Athena that."

"And you think that matters? You think sex is the only thing that makes a relationship an affair? And anyway, how did Athena find out? Did you tell her?"

"I didn't have to. She followed us one day. Can you believe that? She actually got in a car and followed us."

"I'd have done the same thing if I thought someone I loved was screwing around on me. And don't fool yourself. So would you."

Darlene stared at her coffee, while Carol clipped a can opener onto a tin of tuna and started to turn it.

"So, is it a boy or a girl?"

Darlene sighed. "It's a girl."

Carol twisted the opener a little harder. "Doesn't that make a difference?"

"Why should that make a difference? I'm still old enough to be its grandmother."

"Don't be ridiculous," Carol said, dumping the tuna into a bowl and whacking a soupspoon of mayonnaise into it. "Lots of men your age have children."

"Yeah, and most of them are dead before the kid's twenty."

"Well, it won't be easy, that's for sure," Carol said, mixing the sandwich filling as if she were whipping the batter of a cake.

"What do you mean by that?" Darlene asked, eyebrows arching, ready for a fight about the pros and cons of lesbian families.

"I mean chasing a kid around is hard work," Carol said. "And what about this other woman, this student of yours? Have you told her yet?"

Darlene hesitated then nodded.

Carol pulled four slices of bread out of the bag, got out a knife and started smearing them with the pulverized tuna mixture. "So it's over then."

Darlene shrugged. "I guess so."

"What do you mean 'you guess so'? You're not actually thinking about leaving Athena?"

Darlene stared at her hands.

"Do you have any idea how hard it is raising a child alone? Have you even thought about what that would do to her?"

"I didn't ask her to get pregnant, Carol."

Carol leaned on the counter and closed her eyes. "That's it. I can't talk about this any more. It's too upsetting."

"Calm down. I didn't say I was going to leave her. Right now I don't know what to do. It's just too much. First Dad, now Mom, now this...I don't know where I'm at these days. I just need some time. Athena understands that."

Carol sliced through the sandwiches and tossed them onto their plates. "Of course she understands that. Of course she'll wait until you make up your goddamned mind. What other choice does she have? She's pregnant, Darlene. She has a child to raise."

Darlene looked up as if she had just remembered something. "Oh God, Carol, I'm sorry. I wasn't thinking. I know this must be hard for you. I know what you went through."

Carol walked over and slammed a sandwich plate in front of her sister. "No you don't. How could you possibly know? You were never around."

Instead of arguing or defending herself, Darlene just stared out the window. "Yeah," she said. "I suppose that's true."

Carol looked at her sister, and all the fight fizzled out of her like hot wind out of a leaky air mattress.

"She was asking for Dad, you know," Darlene said, her eyes still focused on some unseen corner of the backyard.

"Who was asking for Dad? What are you talking about?"

"The doctor told me. When they brought Mom into the hospital. She was asking when Dad would be up to see her."

There was no way Carol was going to have this conversation, so she picked up her sandwich and walked to the kitchen door.

"Do you think she loved him, Carol?"

Carol pretended she hadn't heard. "I'm going upstairs. You can organize Mom's room."

Carol trudged up the narrow staircase that led to the attic bedroom she had once shared with her sister.

By the time she had arrived at the hospital, her mother hadn't been asking for her father. She had been yelling about dinner.

"What do you have to do to get some food in this place?" she said in a voice loud enough to wake the dead.

"For God's sake, Mother, calm down or you'll give yourself another stroke."

Her mother set her chin like a five-year-old who didn't want to go to bed. "I don't need to calm down. I need to get the hell out of here. I still don't know what they're keeping me here for."

"I told you. They're keeping you in for observation. They want to make sure you're all right before they release you."

"Bloody stupid," Pearl said, folding her arms across her blue cotton hospital garb. "There's nothing wrong with me. I'm perfectly fine."

Carol glanced at her watch, wondering how much longer she'd have to stay, when a silver cart rumbled up to the door. A woman in a hair net stuck her head inside.

"Suppertime," she said in a cheerful voice. "What can I get you, hon? We got roast chicken or pasta and meat sauce tonight."

Carol watched in amazement as her mother offered the woman a sweet smile. "Well, now," she said. "A little chicken might be nice. What does it come with?"

"Mashed potatoes, green peas and a peach cobbler for desert. The cobbler's pretty good tonight."

"That'll suit me fine, thank you."

The woman rolled her mother's table into place, slid a tray off her trolley and placed it in front of her. "Enjoy your dinner," she said and wheeled the trolley back into the hall.

Pearl frowned. "That woman reeked of smoke," she said and peeled the aluminum foil off the tray. Carol winced as her mother stuck her finger into the mashed potatoes.

"Cold as a fridge" she said, licking her finger and pointing at the chicken. "And look at that. That gravy looks like a goddamned jellied salad. She probably loaded up that trolley of hers and went out for a smoke. That dinner's been sitting for at least half an hour."

Carol closed her eyes, counted to five and rolled them open again. "I can call her back if you want. Maybe they've got a microwave on the floor."

"Oh, never mind that," her mother said with a wave of her hand. "I'm so damned hungry I'll eat it as is."

Carol glanced at her watch again. She'd only been visiting for an hour, but dinnertime gave her the perfect excuse. She got to her feet, and Pearl looked up from a forkful of grey peas.

"Can't wait to leave, eh? Well, off you go then. I don't suppose I need you here anyway."

Carol stared at her mother and bit back the temptation to yell. She knew she would be perfectly justified in telling her mother off, but she was damned if she was going to let Pearl provoke her. Knowing her mother, she'd probably have a massive heart attack and die just for the sheer pleasure of leaving Carol behind to writhe in guilt for the rest of her life.

Carol picked up her purse and headed for the door. "I'll see you tomorrow. I'll be by around three."

She was almost out the door when her mother called out after her. "Hold on a second, Carol."

Carol turned around to find her mother frowning at her dinner plate. Her fingertips rested on the too-high surface of the bed table, and her blue hospital gown billowed loose on her neck and arms. She looked so small, so frail and old that the fear Carol had felt on the endless drive up to the hospital came back on her in a sudden roar. Her knees felt weak, and she reached out to press her hand against the doorframe.

Then Pearl looked up, waved her hand in a dismissive gesture and picked up her fork. "Oh, never mind," she said, stabbing a piece of chicken. "I don't want to hold you up."

Carol turned back to the door, her knees once again locked in the comfortable grip of indignation.

Now she stood on the landing outside her childhood bedroom.

Since Pearl's stroke, Darlene had been asking all sorts of questions about their mother's past, picking at it like a scab. Carol didn't care if Pearl had loved their father. If she had loved him, she'd had a pretty lousy way of showing it. Their father had deserved better, a whole lot better, just like Darlene's partner, Athena. If Darlene decided to leave Athena alone and pregnant, Carol knew where her allegiance would lie. Even though the baby wouldn't be Darlene's biological child, she would still be a product of their union, and that was good enough for Carol. That baby would be her niece whether Darlene liked it or not.

She was thinking about all the pretty dresses she could buy when she finally reached the bedroom door and opened it. On the wall opposite the door, the twin beds were positioned where they had always been, one on either side of the small dormer window. They'd been stripped down to the mattresses, and stuck to one of the pink vinyl headboards was a price tag. Carol shook her head. Who would want to buy these old things? The mattresses had to be at least forty years old, and they smelled like the rest of the room, like shrunken mothballs and stale, musty air.

Carol walked over to the window, opened the slats of the Venetian blinds and yanked up on the bottom of the old wooden frame until it gave. She breathed in the fresh summer air, sat down on the edge of one of the beds and opened the drawer of the nightstand that sat between them. It was filled with junk. Two electrical fuses, two old balls of yarn and a stack of scratch pads. She shut the drawer. It could all go to the Sally Anne as far as she was concerned. She got up and walked over to the bureau. In the top drawer, she was surprised to find a stack of her favourite childhood clothing: a pair of baby doll pajamas, the colours faded from repeated washings, two moth-eaten sweaters, both of them blue, and an Indian cotton shirt with pastel flowers embroidered along the neckline. Under the clothing, she found an empty package of cigarettes, and below that, nestled in the powdery remnants of baby's breath, the shattered petals of a long-dead rose.

She slammed the drawer shut and opened the next one. It was filled with Darlene's things, so she closed that as well and bent down to open the bottom drawer. Under a stack of laundered rags, she found two large dress boxes, each with her mother's careful printing on the top. One of the boxes had her name on it, the other one Darlene's.

Reaching in, she pulled out the box with her name printed on it, sat down cross-legged on the floor and opened the lid. A picture slid out from the top of the pile: Carol at eighteen, wearing a long, empire-waist wedding dress, its yards of draped skirt still not full enough to hide the bulge of her pregnancy. Her parents stood on either side of her: her father, big teeth popping out of a wide grin, his arm around what was left of her waist. Her mother on the other side, body held away from Carol's, dark circles around her eyes, her face strained into what looked like a stiff-smiled fury, and on her chest a single red rose pinned to a white satin ribbon. Carol stared at the picture, ripped it in two and shredded it into tiny pieces, just as she had shred all other evidence of that day. She watched the tiny fragments drift to the floor like bits of coloured confetti, then plunged her hand back into the box.

What other nasty tidbits had her mother saved? What other things could she shred?

Her grade eleven photograph came up next: Carol in her favourite dress from The Unicorn, long brown hair resting on her shoulders, lips pressed together in a closed-mouth smile. Carol laid it on the floor beside her and turned back to the box. She flipped through the top layer of paper and was surprised to discover that her mother had kept all of her old school photographs. She'd also kept her report cards, a stack of crayon-coloured drawings, a Dick and Jane workbook and a dot-to-dot book Carol had when she was six. And there were dozens of cards scattered through the pile: Mother's Day and Christmas greetings from Carol to her parents, birthday cards her parents had given to her. She flipped one open and read the verse:

"Your sunny smile is welcome / at the end of every day. / Your happy nature charming, / in oh so many ways. / You are the perfect daughter, / and that is why we say, / We wish you every happiness, / on this your special day!"

It was sweet and corny just like her father, but when Carol looked at the card more closely, she could see that both parents' names had been signed by her mother. She closed the card and studied the illustration on the front: a little girl in a pink and yellow dress dusted with sparkles, and floating over her head a banner that read, "Happy Birthday Eight Year Old."

Well, that made sense. Her mother hadn't had too much to complain about when Carol was eight. She looked at the card again and an unexpected sadness almost swallowed her whole, so she tossed the card onto the growing pile beside her and slid her hand deeper into the box. Her fingers wrapped around a familiar shape and pulled it out. A small square book with a tiny, heart-shaped lock, and on the front the words "My Diary" and the date, "1971": the year Carol got pregnant.

Carol stared at the cover. She was sure she had boxed up all of her old diaries before she left home. As far as she knew, they were all stored in a carton in her basement. How had she managed to leave this one behind?

Carol ran her thumb over the symbols on its cover: a raised heart with little gold studs, psychedelic peace signs, rainbows and doves. There was a folded piece of scratch pad paper sticking out of the diary, secured between the pressed locked pages. Carol pulled it out and opened it.

"I never did read it," the note said. Signed, "Mom."

No "Dear Carol." No "Love, Mom." Just "Mom."

Carol crumpled the note into a ball and threw it across the room, but it was so light that the breeze from the open window caught it and blew it back to her. She watched as it dropped and skittered across the floor, coming to rest against the frosted blue nail of her big toe. Carol stared at the ball of paper.

There was no escape and no way to shorten the distance between them.

On the floor in front of her, horizontal lines of shadow and light ran like ladder steps in the space between the two beds. Carol looked up, and the Venetian blind on the dormer window began to rock back and forth, propelled by the soft summer wind. And as the ladder of light swayed, Carol hung on, hung on as if her very life depended upon it, until she heard the sound of footsteps pounding up the stairs and her sister's voice calling out to her from the doorway.

"You have to see this, Carol," she said. "I found it in her room."

Carol looked up at her sister and began to wail.

CHAPTER 8

1971

"And another thing," Pearl said as she turned to the kitchen counter, broke an egg into a pound of ground beef and dusted it with half a cup of breadcrumbs. "Don't be doing it in a car on the front street where everyone can see you. I'd rather you did it in the house. I don't want the goddamned neighbours gossiping about either one of you."

Carol snuck a look at her sister. Darlene rolled her eyes and shrugged.

Sometimes their mother was a terrifying mystery. Today she was itemizing the rules of dating and, as usual, she was being very specific about what she wanted. The only problem was neither of them could figure out exactly what she meant.

"Okay, Mom," they said in unison.

The ensuing silence indicated that their mother was finished delivering what they privately referred to as her

"Pearls of wisdom."

Darlene raised an eyebrow at Carol and pointed upstairs.

"I guess she doesn't want us necking in a car," Carol said, throwing herself onto the twin bed in the attic bedroom she shared with her sister.

"Well, I don't think she meant that you and Phil should be fucking on the living room couch," Darlene said as she flopped onto her own bed and extended her hand. "Pass me an emery board, will you? My nails are a mess."

Carol frowned as she opened the drawer of the nightstand that sat between their two beds, fished out a nail file and tossed it at Darlene. Ever since her older sister had seen the movie *Woodstock*, the mother of all swear words had become an essential part of her vocabulary. Carol hated the word, but she knew that Darlene loved it because it made her sound tough and cool. But she never used it in front of their mother. Darlene wasn't that cool, and she definitely wasn't that tough.

Carol pushed her pillow up against the pink vinyl headboard and stretched her short, tanned legs down the length of the bed. The room was stifling hot, so she wound her long dark hair into a knot to get it off her neck. Darlene was grinding the emery board against the nail of her left index finger as if she were sawing on the limb of a tree.

"Do you have to do that in here?" Carol snapped.

"What the fuck is wrong with you?" Darlene asked, moving on to file yet another nail with equal force.

"I hate that sound! It's worse than clipping your toenails. Go do it in the bathroom," Carol said, a little louder than she'd intended.

Darlene threw her legs off the bed, stomped over to the

dresser, snagged a bottle of pink frosted and slammed the bedroom door behind her.

When she was gone, Carol went over to the bureau next to the door, opened the top drawer, and slid a package of cigarettes out from under one of her old bras. She walked over to the basket chair next to the open window, lit a cigarette and blew the smoke out the screen, where it curled around the leaves of the Manitoba maple tree and drifted into space.

There was no way her mother could know, she thought as she exhaled cigarette smoke into a spider's web in the corner of the window. A small spider stirred from the heart of the web and ran to the edge of its snare, checking to make sure that the smoky breeze hadn't pulled anything loose. Then it scuttled back to wait for its next meal to fly in. It reminded Carol of the verse her mother had read to her as a child, the one she had learned by heart because it scared her to death and she loved it.

"Come into my parlour," said the spider to the fly.

Carol pushed at the web with her finger, and the spider curled itself into a ball, held on tight and waited. Carol sat back in her chair. Her mother was like that spider – patient, watchful and deadly when she needed to be. She just seemed to know things as if she had a sixth sense, like she could actually feel the slightest emotional draft wafting through Carol's life.

That was why Carol didn't keep her diary in her room any more. If her mother suspected anything, she'd tear the room apart and find it. So Carol kept it under lock and key in a hole she'd spotted in the eaves, just above the workshop her father had built onto the garage. It was one of the few places Carol could be alone, and it was easy to get to. All you had to do was shimmy up the maple tree to its lowest branch, then jump across a foot of open air and onto the flat roof.

Carol hated the fact that her parents' house was so small. She hated fighting with Darlene for the bathroom. Hated being able to hear her parents' voices through the heat duct that ran from their bedroom into hers. But most of all, she hated feeling ashamed of the house because she knew she was being a snob. And Carol hated snobs, which meant she hated most of the girls at her new high school and all the other junior sales clerks at the Hudson's Bay department store.

Carol got up, stretched across her sister's bed and turned on the pink and chrome transistor radio that sat on the nightstand. The opening riffs of "Black Magic Woman" danced out of the tiny speaker. Carol rolled off the bed, sat down in the basket chair, took another drag off her cigarette and leaned back to listen. It was Phil's favourite song, and Carol liked to imagine that he thought about her when he listened to it.

Carol hugged her legs up to her chest and felt the damp, tight fabric of her blue jean cut offs pull against the inside of her thighs. The sensation reminded her of Phillip's fingers, so she closed her eyes and tried to remember every detail. But the memories rushed by, as they always did, in rapid fragments.

The summertime field behind the vocational school grown thick and high with whisker grass, Phil's hand in hers and suddenly he's sitting on the ground, pulling her down toward him. He smells like peppermint and fresh air and his lips are as soft as water. His hand slides across her breasts, her thighs, pulling at her, rocking her until she moans in that mad mixture of fear and pleasure, guilt and delight. Then he's lying on top of her, pushing, and she can feel him through the hard fabric of his Levis, so she lifts her bottom up off the ground and pushes her hips against him. His head lifts up to the sky. He shudders, falls across her, and lies so still she can feel his heart pounding like a bird against her rib cage.

Then he spoils it all by rolling off her, fishing out his Drum tobacco pouch and pulling out a joint.

Carol watched him, sucking the smoke deep into his lungs. Why did he do this? Why did he always get stoned? He was the most beautiful boy Carol had ever dated. He had long blond hair, a small gold hoop in his ear and a face as fine as a girl's. His family lived in a big house and had lots of money. Carol didn't understand why he wanted to escape all of that, just as she didn't understand why he wanted to drift away on a cloud of marijuana every time he got close to her. It made her feel as if she were never enough, could never love him enough, when she loved him so much it sometimes made her crazy. So she watched as he lay back and blew smoke rings into the air, wondering why he had chosen her over all the other girls.

"Take me home," she said, getting to her feet.

"What's the rush?" he asked, his voice dreamy, his eyes rolling and floating in their sockets, his body languid as a snake's lying in the sun.

"I want to leave."

"Oh, come on, Carol," he said, pulling on her hand until she sat down beside him again. "You know I love you."

"Carol!" her mother shouted up the stairs. "Put that bloody cigarette out and get a move on. You're going to be late."

Carol stared at her cigarette. *How did she know?* she wondered as she stubbed the butt into the dirtiest corner of the windowsill, pushed it out a hole in the screen then turned to the closet to get out her work clothes.

Carol raced down the stairs to find her mother standing at the door, waiting for her, hands behind her back, a scowl on her face.

"Are you coming straight home after work?" she said, positioning herself between Carol and the rest of the world.

"I don't know."

"I'm worried about you, Carol. I don't like that boy."

"What's wrong with him? Why do you keep saying that?"

"Because he's a bum. The only thing that boy cares about is that goddamned motorcycle of his." Pearl pulled something out from behind her back and handed it to Carol. "Here. Your father fished it out for me. I was going to read it, but I decided I better not."

Carol snatched the diary out of her mother's hand. "You're disgusting," she said, pushing past her and yanking the door open.

"You watch your mouth, young lady," her mother shouted as she tore out the door behind her.

Carol ran onto the street, clutching her purse and diary to her chest like they were the only things she had left in the world. And as she ran, she could hear her mother's voice shouting after her.

"You can hate me all you want, Carol, but don't you dare come crying to me when you get into trouble. You'll get no sympathy from me!"

Carol got to the stop just as the Logan bus was pulling in. She was so hot she could barely breathe. The long sleeves of her white blouse were pasted against her arms and dark rings were forming on the sleeveless green jacket of her junior sales clerk uniform. She trudged up the stairs of the bus, still clutching her diary, dropped a quarter into the change box and spotted a seat by a window. She sat down and shoved the window open as far as it would go. When the bus started up again, the breeze rushed in to cool her down, and Carol stared at her diary. It didn't really matter if her mother had read it. She wasn't stupid enough to have written down all the details. Still, if she had read it, there were a few things her mother could use against her, like the fact that her friend Gail had already lost her virginity. Technically, Carol was still a virgin, but her mother wouldn't care about that. She'd just assume that where Gail had gone, Carol would eventually follow.

And it was all so stupid anyway. As if you really "lost" your virginity. As if it were something you accidentally dropped on the street and could find again if you just looked for it. Once it was gone, it was gone, and there was no getting it back. But Carol wasn't sure how much longer she could hold out. She wanted Philip as much as he wanted her.

Carol shoved the diary back into her purse and looked at her watch. It was just four thirty. She'd have enough time to tidy up and grab a burger and fries in the employee cafeteria. It was better than the slop her mother served. In fact, as far as Carol was concerned, the cheap food in the employee cafeteria was the best part of her job at the Bay.

Carol hadn't always felt that way. When she first got the news that she'd been chosen as the junior sales clerk for her school, she'd been thrilled and rushed home to tell her mother and father.

"They train us to sell things, and they even teach us how to model," she explained at the dinner table that night. "We do two fashion shows right in the store. I might even get my picture in the paper."

"Well, that's just great, honey," her father said.

"Do they pay you?" her mother asked.

Carol nodded. "And I get an employee discount, so I can even start buying my own clothes."

"Thank the Lord for that," her mother said, getting up from the table and carrying the apple crisp from the counter.

"A model is nothing more than a glorified clothes horse," Darlene sniped. "It's demeaning."

"You're just jealous because I've got a job," Carol snapped back.

"Yeah right. That's just what I want to do, Carol. Prance around in a pair of hot pants."

"Cut it out, you two!" Pearl boomed from the end of the table. "I'm sick of your bickering. Just eat your food, for God's sake."

Carol put her head down and shoved her spoon into her dessert. Her father reached over and patted her arm.

"You should be proud of this, Carol. Real proud."

And Carol had been proud, at least until the day they'd assigned all the junior sales clerks to their departments. Carol watched as all the other girls went to first-floor cosmetics, fifth-floor china and sixth-floor junior miss, while she got stuck in women's clothing in the bargain basement. She'd felt like Cinderella – the poor girl who had to be hidden in the cellar, a grubby place filled with grubby people who all looked green under the flickering fluorescent lights. Her boss, Mrs. Goodman, had bleached blond hair with dark roots, and her bunions pushed out the sides of her spike-heeled shoes. And all the clothes they put out on the racks came packed in crackling cellophane, with plastic hangers, in boxes marked "Taiwan."

Carol was humiliated by it, so humiliated that she couldn't even be happy when she was chosen to have her picture taken for the Dollar Day ad in the newspaper. It was just one more thing to be embarrassed about.

"There goes the Dollar Day queen," she heard one of the other junior sales clerks whisper to a friend. They'd laughed then veered away to take the up escalator, while Carol headed for the down.

Carol looked out the bus window, pushed her hair back and pulled at the front of her shirt, trying to create enough of a breeze to dry the perspiration running down her chest. The bus stopped at a red light, and as she fanned herself, she heard the high-pitched piston whine of a motorcycle pulling up in the next lane.

Maybe it was Phil. Maybe he'd come by to see if he could give her a lift. She'd love to get off this stinking hot bus, that was for sure.

Carol craned her neck around, but what she saw snapped her head back and hunched her down into her seat. It was Phil, all right, and he had another girl on the back of his motorcycle. Carol just sat there, staring at the shiny bald head of the old man in the seat in front of her, then turned back to the window and stuck her head out. The air was so hot she could see it undulating along the pavement, and the exhaust fumes from the cars almost blocked her view, but she could see the girl on the back of the motorcycle. She had long black hair, and she wore a paisley Indian cotton shirt that billowed in the hot wind, but Carol couldn't see her face because she was leaning it against Phillip's back.

The bus lurched forward, and Carol's stomach heaved. She felt sick. Furious. Stupid. She felt like clawing that girl's eyes out. She wanted to get off the bus and beg Phil not to go wherever he was going with that girl. How could he do this? How could he just drive by with someone else while she was on this shithole of a bus in the middle of downtown going to a job she hated? After all the things she'd done for him. After all the things he'd said.

She'd have to get off the bus. She'd have to call in sick. She couldn't face all of those hideous women dressed in their lime-green polyester pantsuits and down-at-the-heel sandals rummaging through the sale bins. Couldn't stand the thought of screaming babies and dirty-fingered children slurping malted milks as they trailed along, hanging on to their mothers' pants. She couldn't face the girls from her old school showing up with their Dippity-dooed hair and their heavy black eyeliner and tacky platform shoes, giggling over a rack of nylon tank tops from the Philippines.

By the time the bus reached Portage Avenue, Carol was so frantic that she almost missed her stop. When she looked up, she found her boss, Mrs. Goodman, standing beside her seat. "This is your stop, Carol," she said. "You don't want to be late for work."

Instead of answering, Carol looked up at her boss and burst into tears.

"They're all shitheads," Mrs. Goodman said as she daubed at Carol's eyes with a paper towel soaked in cold water. "They follow their dicks around, not their heads."

"But he told me he loved me, and I believed him."

"Well, he would say that, wouldn't he? That's how they get what they want. There," Mrs. Goodman said, turning

Carol around to face the mirror. "Good as new."

Carol's face crumpled as she stared at her mascara-smeared eyes and red nose.

"Now cut that out," Mrs. Goodman said, gripping her shoulders. "He's not worth it. Look at you. You're a pretty girl. You're an A student. You've got a great job. You don't need him. You don't need a man any more than I do."

The more indignant she got, the more Mrs. Goodman's back-combed bangs bobbed up and down on her brow, and the sight of this blowzy, red-lipped older woman with her bleached blond hair and black eyebrows finally brought a smile to Carol's lips.

"That's better," Mrs. Goodman said, looking at her watch "Now, it's five thirty. You go on in and get yourself something to eat. Just be on the floor by six. That's soon enough."

Mrs. Goodman charged off, and Carol wandered into the cafeteria. The smell of greasy fries and burgers made her feel sick again, so she walked past the hot food to the dessert display. She had a choice between green Jell-O, cherry pie and bread pudding drowned in a congealed caramel sauce. Carol opted for the Jell-O, got herself a cup of coffee, paid the cashier and found a seat at the back of the room.

She slid some Jell-O into her mouth and held it there until it started to melt. In the six months she'd worked with Mrs. Goodman, the older woman had done little more than bark orders at her, but tonight she'd treated her as a friend. Carol could hardly believe her ears when Mrs. Goodman told her she'd been married and divorced three times. That was almost as many times as Elizabeth Taylor. No wonder she didn't like men. She must have been married to some real duds.

But while she had now decided that she liked Mrs. Goodman, Carol didn't necessarily believe everything she had to say about men. Not all of them were like her three husbands. Her dad wasn't like that, and Phillip wasn't really like that either. She wasn't even sure he was cheating on her. Maybe he'd just been giving that girl a lift. Everybody wanted to ride on a motorcycle, and Phil loved to take all kinds of people out for a spin.

Carol stared at the shivering green gelatin in her parfait glass and decided she'd assume the best until proved wrong. Besides, there was nothing else she could do at the moment. For the next three hours she had to work, and she wouldn't be able to do that if she was crying all over the clothing racks. The next time she saw Phillip she'd ask him who the dark-haired girl was and hope for the right answer. Hope that the dark-haired girl wasn't the black magic woman in Phil's favourite song.

At nine thirty-five, Carol was walking past the main floor perfume counter on her way to the front door of the store. The air, a thick cloud of Estée Lauder mixed with White Shoulders and Evening in Paris, was giving her a headache. Her heart was racing again, and her stomach felt like she'd swallowed a handful of metal shavings. All night long she'd managed to keep her mind on her work, but once her shift was over all she could think about was that girl. She was so preoccupied that she almost missed her turn getting into the revolving door. Its outer edge hit her on the backside, and she stumbled forward into the boy who'd gotten in just before her. He turned around and grabbed her arm.

"Are you okay?" he asked, shuffling his feet sideways

and pushing the glass door with his shoulder to keep it moving.

"I wasn't looking where I was going," Carol said, taking baby steps beside him until they managed to stumble out onto the pavement.

"You work here, don't you?" the boy said.

"Yeah. In women's clothing," Carol replied, careful to avoid mentioning that she worked in the basement.

"I see you in the cafeteria sometimes. I work there," the boy said, leaning his back against the side of the building and lifting his right foot to the wall. He pulled a package of cigarettes out of his back pocket and flipped open a Zippo lighter.

"You want one?" he said, offering her a cigarette. Carol slid an Export A out of the package. The boy cupped the lighter in his hand and leaned in to light her cigarette.

"I'm Gary," he said.

"Carol." She took a long drag off her cigarette, then turned to scan the street to see if Phillip had come to give her a ride home.

"You want to go for a coffee or something, Carol?"

Carol turned back to look at the boy. He was tall and thin, and he had the sweetest smile. But he had strange frizzy hair and acne, and he was dressed in a plaid shirt and grimy jeans, and his hands were red and raw from washing dishes. He reminded Carol of the boys who lived in her neighbourhood.

"Thanks," she said, "but my boyfriend's picking me up."

"Sure. No problem." Gary shrugged, pushing his back off the wall. "Catch you later."

Carol watched the boy walk away. He looked good

from behind, walking with an easy, comfortable stride. Maybe she should have gone out with him. They could have gone to the Parkway coffee house where Phillip hung out. She would have enjoyed seeing the look on his face. It would have served him right.

When Carol got off the bus at the top of her street, she could see him sitting on his motorcycle, waiting for her.

"Hey," he said as she walked down the sidewalk.

"What are you doing here?" she said, striding past without looking.

She heard him kick out the bike stand and start the engine. She was three houses down the street when he finally caught up with her. He swerved in, putting his foot out on the curb to steady the motorcycle, and followed along beside her.

"Jesus, Carol, what's with you? Get on the bike."

"I saw you today. Who was the girl?"

"What are you talking about?"

"I saw you. You were driving downtown with another girl on the back of the bike. So who is she?"

"She's a friend."

Carol snorted. "Some friend."

"We use the same dealer, Carol. I was giving her a lift. That's it. And even if it wasn't, what's the big deal? It's not like we're married or something."

Carol stopped dead in her tracks and turned to look at him. "Go to hell," she said.

Phil pushed his bike away from the curb, gunned it twice and did a wheelie down the street.

Carol watched him roar away, then turned to stare up at her dark, empty house. It was Friday night. Her sister was out, her dad was probably at the legion and her mother was catering. Carol headed up the walk, sat down on the front steps and looked at her watch. If he wasn't back in fifteen minutes, she'd go in the house, call Gail and see if there was a party on somewhere. She couldn't bear the thought of sitting in the living room alone.

Carol hugged her purse into her lap and felt the hard edge of her diary push into her bottom rib. Why did he have to be like this? Why did he have to make her feel so cheap?

It's not like we're married or something.

Well, maybe they weren't married, but their bodies acted as if they were. Their bodies knew that they were meant for one another. It was their fate. Two hearts caught, like flies in a web.

Five minutes later, Phil pulled up on his bike. He switched the engine off, swung his right leg over the seat, leaned on the motorcycle and looked at her. "She's nobody," he said. "She's not important."

Carol stared at his tanned face, his sun-bleached blond hair and his baby-blue jean shirt rolled up on his forearms. He looked like a cowboy, like a gun-slinging outlaw.

And the sudden recognition of who he was and what he wanted came upon her like a cool breeze. Despite the heat, she shivered because she knew what she had to do. She knew what she had to do to keep him away from that other girl.

She pulled her keys out of her purse and dangled them in front of her face. They tinkled like wind chimes brushed by a warm summer wind. Carol smiled, raised her other hand and beckoned him toward her.

CHAPTER 9

2000

It was nine o'clock by the time Darlene got home from the hospital. She let herself in the front door, dropped her keys on the hall table and stopped to listen, hoping that Athena had changed her mind and would call out from the kitchen as she so often did when Darlene arrived home late. But the only sounds were the hum of the air conditioner and the dull thud of her own shoes as she walked down the hallway into the living room. The boxes from her mother's house were still sitting on the couch where she'd left them. One large and one small: boxes filled with photographs and mementoes, filled with her mother's secrets.

Darlene opened her purse and slid a small black and white photograph from the inside pocket. A little girl sat on a horse, nestled against her father's chest and legs. Beside the horse, holding the reins, stood a skinny woman with tightly curled blond hair, and in the distance, next to a stand of trees, the short, squat body of what appeared to be a man.

"Who are these people?" she had asked, holding up the photograph for her mother to see.

Pearl grabbed her reading glasses off the bedside table, took the photo from Darlene and peered at it. "Where the hell did you get this?" she asked, eyebrows raised over the edge of her narrow frames.

"In your room. When Carol and I were tidying up."

"You were supposed to be organizing, not going through my things," her mother said as she whipped off her glasses and folded them shut with a click. "You had no business doing that. And besides, you know perfectly well who that is. It's a picture of you and your father. You must be about three."

"Who's the woman?"

Pearl thrust the picture at her. "Your father's sister, Jolene."

Darlene frowned at the photograph. "He didn't talk about her much, did he?"

"Well, he wouldn't, would he? By the time you'd have noticed, she was long gone. She died about a year or two after that was taken, in fact."

"How did she die?"

Pearl shrugged and fiddled with the tie on the front of her hospital gown. "Drunk, I suspect. Wrapped her car around a telephone pole."

Darlene pointed at the picture. "And who's that over there, by the tree in the background?"

Pearl's eyes closed up like two blue doors. "How the hell should I know, Darlene? I didn't keep track of Jolene's friends. Besides, I didn't go out there much."

"Why, Mom? Didn't you like her?"

Pearl lay back against her pillows. "That's enough, Darlene. I'm tired now. I need to rest."

Darlene sat down on the chair at the end of her

mother's bed and stared at the photograph. Maybe this had been a mistake. Maybe she should've just left it alone and done what her mother had done. Left the past to the dead. Maybe she should just go down to the cafeteria, get herself a coffee and forget about it.

She got to her feet and was heading for the door when her mother spoke again.

"That other person in the photograph," she said, staring out the window. "That's my older sister, Winnie."

Darlene carried the boxes from the living room to her office, set them on her desk and walked over to the sliding doors. The grass of the upper yard was lush and green, and the river beyond its boundaries ran slow and heavy with silt, its shallow bottom permanently hidden from view. Darlene stared at the river, imagining all of the strange things that might be hidden in its muddy depths or swimming through its murky waters: massive sturgeons as large as any swordfish, rotting canoes, rusted-out cars and myriad farm implements washed into its bowels when the snow melted and the river swelled, thundering over its banks, ripping out trees, flooding houses, swallowing up everything in its path.

She and Athena had sandbagged for two weeks that spring, fighting the threatening flood by extending the height of the riverbank another three feet into the air. But in the hidden lower part of the yard, the water swept over the barrier, drowning wildflowers and prairie grass, leaving behind a four-inch layer of powdery white silt that dried and cracked in the heat of the sun like badly poured concrete. The shoreline was a moonscape now, and Darlene had raged for weeks.

"I can't even look at it," she said. "I loved sitting down there, and now it's a bloody mess."

"It'll come back," Athena said, walking to the edge of the grass and peering down. "With all that rich soil, it's bound to come back."

Darlene shook her head. "It's not soil, Athena, it's gumbo. And it's full of chemical pesticides and crap."

Athena had turned to look at her with one of her more enigmatic smiles, then disappeared over the rise and down the path that led to the river.

Darlene turned away from the window and sat down at her desk. Earlier that day, when she came through the door, carrying the boxes from her mother's house, she had found Athena on the living room couch with a large suitcase sitting on the floor beside her.

"I'm going to stay with Cindy," she said, getting to her feet. " She's picking me up in a few minutes. I was going to leave you a note, but I thought that wouldn't be fair, so I decided to wait for you."

Athena lifted the handle of her suitcase and rolled it toward the door. Darlene dumped the boxes onto the couch and hurried after her.

"But why? What are you doing, Athena? Why are you leaving?"

Athena shook her head. " I know it's not the best time to do this, and I know I said I would wait, but I can't. I have the baby to think about. And you need to decide whether you want us here or not."

Darlene reached out and grabbed her arm. "But I told you, Thena. I'm not seeing her any more."

A car horn tooted outside. Athena pulled her arm away and reached for the door. "Just because you're not seeing her doesn't mean you're not thinking about it," she said and hoisted her suitcase over the doorframe and onto the stoop.

"Please, Athena. Tell her I'll drive you over later. I'll drop you off on my way to the hospital. I found all this stuff at Mom's house. I need to talk about it."

"Talk to your mother about it, Darlene. I have to leave," Athena said and closed the door behind her.

Darlene stared at the boxes, fighting the urge to cry just as her sister had cried when she found her sitting on the floor of their old attic bedroom. She hadn't known what to do when Carol started to wail. She hadn't held her sister, hadn't hugged or even touched her in so many years that the thought of it terrified her. But when she forced herself to walk over, bend down and reach out, Carol hadn't pulled back or pushed her away. Instead, she had clung to her, and the only thing Darlene felt was relief, as if she'd been forgiven for every sin she had ever committed.

"Why is she always so angry at me?" Carol howled.

Darlene ran her hand down the rounded back of Carol's head, rested it on the tender nape of her neck and watched her own tears disappear like warm rain into the strands of her sister's hair.

"I don't know, Carol," she said. "I don't know."

Darlene opened the larger of the two boxes and began sorting through its contents: a packet of letters, a pocket watch, an old uniform, a pair of scissors, a grubby old rag rug and a small book of poems. She flipped open the front cover of the book and read the signature: *Matthew McKay, 1941, Aldershot.* Darlene closed it and did what she often did when she was curious about a used book she thought she might buy. She held it by the spine, fingers closed around the front, her thumb on the back cover, then slowly opened her hand to see where the book would fall open and what it might reveal about the mind that had once held it. Darlene scanned the open page and a poem by Matthew Arnold. The last few lines had been underlined in soft, black pencil: "For the world, which seems / To lie before us like a land of dreams / So various, so beautiful, so new / Hath really neither joy, nor love, nor light / Nor certitude, nor peace, nor help for pain…"

Darlene closed the book, stared out at the river and thought about time and all of the lives that lay buried in her mother's past, buried like the artifacts at the bottom of the muddy water that flowed outside her window.

"So they lived together?" she asked.

Her mother nodded.

"Were they a couple?"

"Oh, for God's sake, Darlene, I don't know. People didn't even think about that kind of thing back then. They were just two women who shared a house."

"Did you *ever* visit them?"

"Once. Just before my sister died."

"But why, Mom? Why didn't you go out and see her more often?"

Pearl shook her head and closed her eyes. "It was a long time ago, Darlene."

Darlene opened the smaller of the two boxes and pulled out a photograph of her mother's family: the grandmother and grandfather she knew nothing about, the aunt and uncle who had both died so young and their sister, her mother, the one who had survived. Winnie and Pearl sat side by side on the porch, Winnie's arm wrapped around her younger sister's shoulder. It was clear that they had loved one another once, and it would have been so easy to speculate about the things that had driven them apart. But Darlene was beginning to understand that life was never that simple. The events that measured the distance between love and disaffection were often too numerous and too complex to ever fully comprehend.

If they weren't, then she would be able to explain the distance between herself and her own sister.

Earlier that afternoon, when Carol's tears were spent, Darlene had led her downstairs to their mother's bedroom. Carol hesitated in the doorway, wrinkling her nose, sniffing at the air.

"It smells like her," she said and walked across the room. Stopping at the vanity opposite Pearl's bed, she picked up a bottle of perfume and read the label. "Simply Rose," she said, pressing the bottle to her nose, then holding it away to stare at it. "They used to call it Wild Rose, remember?" Carol set the candy-coloured perfume back in its place, sat down on the edge of the bed and folded her arms. "So what did you want me to see?"

Darlene picked up the two cardboard boxes and placed them on the bed next to her sister.

"What's this?"

"Open it," Darlene said, pointing at the shoebox.

Carol opened the lid and stared at the pile of photographs. She reached in, picked up a family portrait and peered at it. "Who are these people?"

Darlene watched as Carol turned the picture over and read the inscription. She flipped it over again, stared at the image and shook her head. "So she lied to us," she said, tossing the photograph back into the box. "She wasn't a poor little orphan girl after all."

"I don't think she lied, Carol. She just didn't tell us everything."

"What's the difference?" Carol said, getting to her feet.

"Don't you want to look at the rest? Aren't you even a little curious?" Darlene looked at her sister's face. The woman who had just cried like a broken-hearted child was gone, and the tight-assed matron had once again taken her place.

"If she couldn't be bothered telling us about her family, why the hell should I care?"

"It might explain a few things."

"What could it possibly explain, Darlene? She's an angry, bitter old woman. And she was a lousy mother. End of story."

Darlene stared down at the grey and white photograph. She could barely make out the child's features, so she rummaged around in her desk drawer until she found a magnifying glass and centred it on the little girl's face. Pearl's hands were folded in her lap, her toe-scuffed lace-up shoes pressed together, her locked knees covered by the hem of her dress. The dress appeared to be made of cotton, with tiny buttons on the bodice, and it looked like a well-worn hand-me-down: the fabric limp and thin, the rounded collar a little too frayed. Above the collar, in a slightly blurred face, defiant eyes stared straight ahead, lips pressed into an unwilling grin as if responding to an unwanted command: "Smile for the birdie."

Darlene set the magnifying glass down and looked at the photographs on her own desk: not one of her parents or sister, just her and Athena and their lesbian friends. Out of the closet but still hemmed in, constrained by all the others who didn't want to see two women holding hands.

"I don't know what the hell's the matter with people these days," her mother had said. "My girlfriends and I always walked arm in arm, and no one gave two hoots. They never thought a thing about it. And nobody gave two hoots about my sister and Jolene. They were just friends."

Darlene got up from her chair, opened the cupboard on the far wall and rifled through the file folders hanging inside. She found what she wanted, walked back to her desk and sat down. Inside the file was a photograph taken the day she married Ben: Darlene surrounded by her bridesmaids, all but one smiling at the camera.

She had felt so serene that day, watching Kathy zip up the back of Joanne's dress, sitting patiently while her mother slid daisies into her upswept hair. Joanne was Darlene's oldest friend, but Kathy was her best, and she looked so beautiful that day, her auburn hair done up in a French twist, the crepe fabric of her seafoam-coloured bridesmaid's dress clinging to her tall, slender body like a Grecian robe. She and Kathy had become friends in grade ten, two would-be hippies who smoked dope, skipped classes together and laughed at the jocks and the hot roller girls who prowled the halls, hunting for boys. Darlene loved Kathy like a sister, and on days like today, as she watched her move about the room in her quiet, competent way, she thought she might love her even more than she loved Ben.

Kathy turned and smiled, and Darlene felt a sense of

contentment so sweet that she never wanted it to end. Then Carol shrieked from the other side of the room, and the brief moment of bliss came to a sudden, crashing end.

"I can't wear this," Carol howled. "It's too tight. I look like a beached whale."

Darlene turned around as her mother tossed a handful of daisies onto the bed and stomped across the room to Carol. Kathy and Joanne hurried after her, and Darlene reluctantly followed. The four of them stared at her sister's silhouette in the full-length mirror that hung on the cupboard door. Carol was seven months pregnant with her second child, and even though they had all gone to their last dress fitting just ten days before, her belly had suddenly mushroomed. It strained against the soft fabric of her bridesmaid's gown like a beach ball stuffed inside a blanket.

Pearl grabbed her by the shoulders and turned her around. "Take the damned thing off. I need to look at the seams."

Darlene watched as Carol slipped the straps off her shoulders, peeled the fabric over her belly and leaned on her mother's bent back to step out of the dress.

Darlene had announced that she was getting married twelve months ago, but that hadn't stopped Carol from getting pregnant again.

"You were pregnant at your own wedding," Darlene said. "Did you have to get pregnant for mine?"

"I didn't plan it this way," Carol said. "It just happened."

Darlene stared at her sister's stretched belly, her huge, pendulous breasts, and swollen ankles and sighed. Telling Carol that she could have used birth control would have been futile.

"I've got about a quarter inch," Pearl said, staring at the inner seams. "That might be enough."

Darlene looked at her watch. "We have to leave in half an hour," she said, pointing at her mother. "And look at you, you're not even dressed. And who's going to finish my hair?" She turned to face her sister. "Can't you just wear it the way it is? It doesn't look that bad."

Carol started to sob. Pearl grabbed her arm, aimed her at the stairs and turned back to face Darlene. "Don't be so damned selfish. The girls can help you finish up. And if you don't show up on time, no one's going anywhere. They'll just bloody well wait."

Pearl disappeared down the stairs, and Darlene trudged back to where she had been sitting. She pointed at the daisies on the bed.

"Who wants to finish sticking those things in my hair?" she asked. Joanne hitched up the bottom of her crepe dress and hurried over.

"Boy. Your mother's really something, isn't she?" Kathy said.

"That's one way of putting it." Darlene winced as Joanne chose a spot in her hairdo and drove a daisy stem into it.

"Well, at least she tells you what she thinks," Joanne said, standing back to assess her limited skill in hair design. "Unlike my mother, who just suffers in mind-numbing silence."

Kathy walked over and pushed Joanne out of the way. "She's starting to look like she's got a flower pot on her head. Go downstairs and see if they need help pulling those seams apart. I'll finish this."

Joanne looked relieved to go. Kathy put her hands on Darlene's shoulders, turned her around to face the vanity mirror and started picking daisies from her hair. Darlene watched as Kathy's long fingers slid through the mass of upswept curls that smothered her head. She looked at her best friend's reflection in the mirror and smiled. "You know how much I love you, don't you? How much I wanted you to be my maid of honour? But I had to ask my sister or my mother would have killed me."

Kathy leaned down, put her own face next to Darlene's and smiled at her reflection in the mirror. "I love you too, Dar."

Something in the tone of her voice frightened Darlene. It was as if someone else had spoken, as if she had just heard the sound of Ben's voice when he turned toward her in bed.

"I can't believe you're getting married. I can't believe you actually said yes."

Darlene fiddled with her makeup bag. "Well, he was never going to stop asking, so I had to say yes."

When she looked up, Kathy's hands reached out to cup her cheeks, and her gloss-coated mouth slid across Darlene's lips like a strangely perfumed cream. "I love you, Darlene," she whispered. "I've always loved you."

Darlene wrenched her body back and pushed her friend away. "Stop it. Stop it right now." She reached for a Kleenex and scrubbed at her lips, but when she looked up into the mirror, she didn't see the monster she expected. She just saw her own face and Kathy's reflection, the image of her best friend, the woman she loved, standing there in a seafoam-coloured bridesmaid's dress, her face white as a chalk stick, looking as if one unkind word from Darlene might topple her.

"Oh God," Kathy whispered. "Don't hate me, Darlene. Please don't hate me."

"Hate you for what?" Carol asked as she lumbered into the room with her bridesmaid's dress still stretched taut across her massive belly.

Darlene's voice was as quiet and lethal as a shard of falling ice. "Get out, Carol. Get your fat, pregnant ass out of here."

Darlene stared down at the photograph.

She had managed to stay married to Ben for two years, and during the first year, Kathy had moved to Toronto. When her marriage to Ben ended, Darlene tried to track her down but heard through mutual friends that Kathy had become a born-again Christian, married a lawyer and gone to Vancouver. One year, out of the blue, she sent Darlene a Christmas card with a nativity scene on the front and a photograph of her family inside. Her substantial, suited husband stood behind her, his hand resting on her shoulder. Kathy sat in a straight-backed chair, plump and frumpy, surrounded by two dark-haired sons and a tall, slender daughter who had her mother's red hair.

God has blessed me, the note at the bottom of the card read. *Love, Kathy*.

Darlene cried when she read those words, wondering what their lives might have been if she had had the courage to seize the moment instead of yelling at her pregnant sister as if her own choices had somehow been Carol's fault, as if her little sister's life had always stood in implicit judgement on hers.

Darlene stared at the faces of her bridesmaids: Joanne beaming on one side, Kathy on the other, smiling bravely as if nothing had happened, and Carol, hiding her body behind them all, trying to smile and failing, staring over Darlene's shoulder like a ghost.

All of her life, Darlene had felt as if she didn't belong, that she was an aberration, an orphan like her mother, with no real blood ties and no family past. But it turned out that her mother did have a past, and Darlene did have a family: the one her mother had kept hidden from her, and the one she had always denied herself.

When Darlene left the hospital, she drove to the other side of town and parked across the street from Georgia's apartment building. She sat in the idling car, staring up at the third-floor window, debating whether she should show up unannounced or call on her cell phone and run the risk of rejection. Ten minutes later, she found herself standing outside Georgia's apartment with her ear pressed to the door. A stereo was on, the bass cranked up, the grinding drone creating a wall of vibrating sound that rattled the doorknob.

Darlene stepped back and leaned against the opposite wall. This was ridiculous. She had to break it off. She had to stop telling lies. In the past few days, she had lied to both her sister and Athena. She hadn't told Georgia about Athena's pregnancy, and she had never suggested that they stop seeing one another. Instead, she had simply avoided taking Georgia's calls, and when she finally did answer, she used her mother's illness as an excuse.

"But I'm leaving in a few days," Georgia said. "I'd like to say goodbye."

"You're only gone for a few weeks. I'll still be here when you get back."

"But I need to see you now. We need to talk."

"Look, I'm sorry about this, really, I am. But right now the only thing I can deal with is my mother."

"Fine. Okay. Maybe I'll see you when I get back, then."

"Georgia, wait, of course you'll see me…" she said, then realized she was speaking into dead air.

Darlene stared at Georgia's door, opened her purse and took out the small box she had been carrying around for days. It was a gift, something she'd had a local jeweller make, after Georgia told her that she would be returning to London for a few weeks to visit her parents. It was a travel charm made up as a pendant: not the usual St. Christopher's medal, not even a charm of Hermes, patron god of travellers. On it was the likeness of a woman, the goddess Hestia, known to the Romans as Vesta, protector of the destination to which every traveler longs to return – guardian of hearth and home.

Clutching the box in her hand, Darlene crossed the hall and rang the bell. No answer. She rang again. This time someone turned the stereo down, and footsteps approached the door. When it opened, a young man named Vince was standing there, a student from Darlene's graduate seminar, the one who always sat beside Georgia, the one who followed her around like a love-starved dog.

His shirt was open, and his jeans rested low on narrow hips. "Professor Calder," he said. "Wow, this is a surprise."

Darlene forced herself to smile. "Is Georgia here, Vince?"

"Yeah, she is, but she's in the tub," he said and laughed, half proud, half embarrassed, his long, dark eyelashes batting against flawless, unlined lids. "Did you want to come in and wait?"

"No, no. It's not important. Just tell her I dropped by. I had a book I wanted to get back from her, but it can wait." Darlene palmed the small gift box and slid it into her pocket.

"Are you sure you won't come in?"

"Yes, Vince. I'm sure. Just tell her to drop the book off at the department when she gets back. The secretary will keep it for me."

"Oh, sure, well...nice seeing you, Professor Calder."

"Nice to see you too, Vince," Darlene said.

Darlene stared through the patio door, trying to imagine what Georgia had felt when she opened the bathroom door and got the message from young Vince. Did she feel guilt? Did she feel anger? Or did she feel what Darlene had felt: a small and tender sorrow, a flowering of relief?

Darlene reached into her pocket, pulled out the gift box and opened it. She lifted the silver chain and the small charm dropped, flaring like a spark as it spun in the air. On impulse, she opened the clasp, put the chain around her neck and fastened it. She turned away from the window, picked up the book of poems that lay open on her desk and read about a calm sea, a light flickering on a distant coast and waves that began and ceased and began again.

When she finished, she got to her feet, slid open the door and stepped outside. The light was muted now, the air fragrant with the smell of blooming flowers and damp grass. It was so quiet at this time of night, quiet and pristine, the very atmosphere tactile, sensual in stillness. Darlene walked down the flagstone path that led to the edge of the yard and stopped. The elm trees on the shoreline, backlit against the dying sun, stood black in silhouette, the last light cutting through their branches, slicing past their massive solid trunks. And below the trees, in the white moonscape of the once drowned shore, sat a single tuft of sturdy prairie grass, its base lit golden in a shaft of light, its sharp green blades transforming radiance into life.

CHAPTER 10

1942

He knows how a bruised rib responds to a weight in his arms, the way a blackened eyelid throbs when he bends down to tie his shoes, what it feels like to stare at a hand, hanging useless at the end of a broken arm. It isn't the physical pain that frightens him. It is the anticipation of it. That split second before a bomb blast. The moment his father froze in his tracks.

Those are the moments of real pain. The rest is just consequence.

There are forty-five men in his platoon, and they are all huddled inside this landing craft. A flat metal box open to the air and the smell of salt and sea, it hits the waves like a two by four. Slam. Slam. The domed sky is moonless, and clouds hide the light of the stars. Somewhere in the distance lie the beaches of France and the men who wait on the other side. He imagines them patrolling the boardwalks, staring up at the same black heaven and wondering, as he does, if they will survive.

He has a book of poems wrapped in a piece of oilcloth to protect it from sea foam and rain. Stuffed inside his jacket, it rests against his heart. He bought it at the bookstore in Basingstoke, where he met Rosie: the only rose that by any other name would always smell as sweet. Yesterday they spent their last night together, and her scent still lingers on his hand.

"Ah, love, let us be true to one another..."

When he finished reading the poem, she rolled over onto her stomach and lifted her eyes. "It's so sad, Mattie. Can't you find a happy one? Something about daffodils and rain?"

He smiled at her then, kissed the top of her head and breathed in the scent of roses.

"Tell me about your family," she said.

"I told you," he said, pulling away from her. "My parents are dead. I've got two sisters. They live with my aunt and uncle now."

"But how did your parents die?"

"In an accident," he said. "A terrible accident," he lied.

When he arrived in England, he thought he had never seen a country so green. It was damp with it, lush with it, and he loved the smell of the water-drenched air so soothing to lungs accustomed to dryness and dust. On a day's leave, he would walk the town of Aldershot or take to the roads to see the sights. In a park, he found a thousand yellow daffodils growing up through the grass, and a tree with waxy pink cups sitting upright at the tips of its branches like fleshy wine goblets where the fairies hid.

And as he walked the countryside, it seemed to him that England was the motherland of fairies, a place where the mist drifted and swirled inside the Devil's Punch Bowl and the New Forest hid strange and ancient creatures. But best of all, England was a land of books: books housed in the libraries of town halls and churches, labour temples and schools.

One of the first books he borrowed was about a Buddhist monk. It described how, in the early days of training, the young initiates sat in a row with their backs to their master. How the master would carry a cane in his hand, walk along behind them and strike without warning. When a young monk could anticipate the blow, when he could sense the master behind him, hear the current of air created by the rising cane, when he could bend his body down before it struck, his training was complete.

And so it was with him.

"I don't know what I'd do without my mother and dad. They're the most important people in my life," Rosie said. "Next to you, of course."

Matthew nodded. "They're good people, your folks."

"My dad says the same thing about you. He says that you're a good man."

Matthew fell silent, wondering at the miracle of this. The miracle of being a good man.

"Tell me what it will be like?"

"Well," he said, leaning back. "We live in a big farm house out on the prairies, and we have three kids, two boys and a girl. And I work the farm, and we sit on the porch in the evening just to look at the sky. It's such a big sky, Rosie, bigger than you've ever seen, and the colours of the setting sun are like a neon sign made by God himself."

"But there's a lot of snow, isn't there? And the winters are long and cold?"

"Never mind," he said, pulling her to him. "I'll keep you warm."

There is no warmth tonight. Out on the open sea, even in August, the cold bites through his clothes and into his skin, cutting its hard, wet teeth into muscle and sinew.

When he was little, his father whipped him with his belt. As soon as he turned thirteen, the old man started pounding him with his fists. The first time it happened, Matthew was reading a book.

"You won't find life in that," his father said, knocking the pages out of his hands and grabbing him by the shirt-front. "It's out there, in the cow shit."

The day he turned fourteen, his father announced that Matthew would not be returning to school. Matthew had begged his father to let him go. He had expected to be beaten for it. Instead, his father just shook his head and walked away.

"I need you here," he said. "That's just the way it is."

For the next three years, Matthew spent every working hour of every day in his father's presence, and in time, he learned to read the signs. The sudden pause when his father stopped walking and looked up at the sky. The way his back tensed, the opening and closing of his empty hands. As time went on, Matthew learned when to speak, when to hold his tongue and when to disappear around the corner of the barn, melting into the sun-scorched fields like a ghost. He learned how to wait. Eventually, he found a way to escape. When war was declared, Matthew signed up and let his father beat him one last time.

"You will not die," his father said as he pounded his fists into Matthew's face. "I will not let you die."

Matthew wipes the salt spray from his eyes and wonders what his father meant. He wonders why a man who did his best to kill him would care whether he lived or died.

"We need loyal men here," the recruiter said. "We need men who love their country."

"I love my country, but I hate those Toronto bastards!" shouted one of the boys a few men down in the line. "Does that mean I can't go?"

Everyone laughed and chimed in their hatred of all things east of Thunder Bay, because they knew the recruiter was a local farmer and wouldn't disagree.

He grinned and shouted back, "You'll do."

But love of country is not the reason Matthew is sitting in this metal tomb tonight.

When he got on the train that would take him to the troop ship in Montreal, his only thought had been of escape: to leave behind the terror of his father's house, his mother's sickness and a dried-out, dying land. His only regret had been leaving his sisters, and the hardest part was leaving Pearl. She was the youngest, a wild and fearless little thing: not quiet and taciturn like Winnie, not closed up and fearful like him.

"Just be nice to Dad," she would say. "He only hits you when you're bad."

And that's the way life was for Pearl. Hers was the black and white universe of a twelve-year-old: be good, and nothing bad will happen. Be fearless, and no one will ever hurt you.

The day before he left, the day his father beat him for the last time, Pearl had argued with him, tried to convince him not to go. "You've got no business leaving," she said as Winnie dabbed his face with a clean rag soaked in peroxide. "Mom needs you. So does Dad."

He stared at her then, pouring his heart and all of his love into his black and swollen eyes so she would know that he wasn't leaving her. She looked back at him, and for the first time, Mattie saw fear winking out like a cold white star from behind the cloud of defiance.

"Go ahead and die, then," she said. "See if I care." She got up and walked out of the house, the screen door banging shut behind her.

"She doesn't mean it," Winnie said.

Mattie winced as the peroxide hit the sliced flesh just below his eyebrow. "I know that, Winnie. I know."

Matthew stares out to sea, marvelling at this great seething mass, this living, breathing being that holds within its body a thousand, thousand other living creatures, and the liquid source of all life beyond its bounds. He remembers the first time he glimpsed it as the troop ship rounded the shores of the St. Lawrence River and struck out for open sea. The same endless emptiness as the prairies, with only a heaving horizon to distinguish them: that and water as far as the eye could see. And day after day the greyness, a slate sky and sea that seemed to go on forever until the sun broke through and the world lit up in every shade of blue: the blue of delphiniums and creek water, the blue of crocuses and bottled ink.

Before the sea voyage, on the long train journey eastward, he saw so many wonders that even when darkness fell, and he huddled against his seat and tried for sleep, the visions kept flashing by: blasted granite walls and windswept trees towering on the cliffs of ancient lakes. Whistle stops where people waited to cheer them on or climbed onto passenger cars to ride on to other distant destinations: big cities, great sprawling giants, dirty backsides turned to the train tracks – handsome faces laughing in all the gilt and glitter of their massive dome-topped stations.

He wrote home every day, one letter for each of the girls and one for his mother. He wrote the return address onto every envelope and waited patiently for Toronto, where they would get off the train to collect their mail. But when he lined up for his letters, he was handed only one thin envelope, a telegram from his Uncle Edward.

MOTHER AND FATHER DEAD STOP GIRLS
WITH US STOP LETTER TO FOLLOW STOP

Matthew ran to his sergeant and asked for permission to call home, but no one answered at his aunt and uncle's place. So he got back on the train and waited until Montreal to find out what had happened.

> *Dear Mattie,*
> *I guess you heard about things by now*
> *from Winnie. Me and her are staying with*
> *Aunt Clara and Uncle Edward. I hate them,*

but I like your storys. I really liked the one
about you and the other boys drinking beer. I
hope you write again real soon.
Your sister,
Pearl

PS: No one will tell me what happened.
Maybe you know, or maybe you can come
home. Winnie really misses you.

He did ask if he could go home, even though he knew
what the answer would be: that once you enlisted, you belonged to the army, no matter what happened to your own
family. And after almost two years in England, the army
had become a kind of family to him, his buddies like
brothers for whom he would lay down his life. They are
all around him now, crowded shoulder to shoulder, each
man straining to catch the first glimpse of land, scanning
the horizon, dreading the sight of that first arcing light. A
light that will rise up into the sky like the burst of a
Roman Candle, then fall, blowing their bodies to
smithereens, sending the pieces hurtling into the night.

None of them speak, because they are under silent running orders. Given the roar of the engines, silence seems
pointless to Matthew, but he and the others do not speak
because they want to live. Instead, they talk with their eyes
and hands, gripping their rifle muzzles tighter, pointing to
a man sick with fear and the sea. They pat his back to give
him comfort, to let him know that he is still alive and in
good company.

His uncle Edward's letter had explained it all. How Winnie had found his parents: his mother lying in bed, a pillow still covering her face, his father hanging from a rafter in the barn. He must have killed her in the hours just before dawn, before Winnie rose to light the stove and cook breakfast. His uncle's letter expressed no sadness, just the angry facts and resentment at having to take Pearl and Winnie into his home. Edward had always hated Matthew's father because he had inherited the farm.

Clara and I always figured it would come to this or something like it. Your father wasn't much good for anything after the last war, and your grandmother was right. He never should have married your mother.

Matthew held his uncle's letter over his dinner plate and lit it with his lighter, watching the pages curl and burn into ash. He felt no satisfaction that his father was dead. He felt only sadness for Winnie, worry for his sister Pearl, and grief. And that was the strangest thing of all: that he felt grief, not just for his poor dead mother but for the man who had beaten him, murdered his wife and then killed himself.

When his uncle's letter was nothing more than a greasy smear on his plate, Matthew got out his pen and wrote a letter to Pearl. He told her to be good and keep her head down. He told her to study hard at school and not talk back. Then he lied and told her that he would be home soon, that they would be a family again. He made no attempt to explain what his father had done, because he could hardly comprehend it himself.

Dear Mattie,
Winnie and me go to the post office every
day to see if there's a letter. It's been a week

*now and still no sign. Hope your ok. I joined
the softball team and I am there number one
batter. You should see how far I can hit. Right
over the fence and into the field. Joe says I'm
the best he ever saw for a girl. He says he's
going to sign up as soon as he can and so is
Henry Calder so maybe you'll see them over
there. I don't know why Joe wants to go but
there it is. I'll just have to wait for him to get
back. Most of the boys in town are gone, but
there's a bunch of new ones up at the new air-
field. Me and Winnie are ok, but I still hate u
know who. Write soon.*
Your sister,
Pearl

During their final training, on the Isle of Wight, Matthew
distinguished himself as a soldier to be reckoned with, and
they promoted him to sergeant. What they didn't know
was how much he enjoyed it. How he loved crawling on
his belly through the mud, climbing the twenty-foot rope
ladders and tumbling down the other side. How he loved
the feel of his blackened face at night as he planned an
ambush then watched the opposing team fall into his trap.
How he loved the feel of his battered body at the end of
the day, and worse, how much he loved to rush those life
sized dummies with his knife, piercing their stuffed bellies
with his blade then yanking it up to finish the job. All the
rage he'd ever felt went into his commando training, and
when he climbed into bed at night he slept like he had
never slept before. He slept the sleep of the dead.

And he couldn't wait for that last boat to come in, the

one that would carry him to Rosie. He'd booked a hotel in town where they would spend their last night together. They were engaged now, and even her parents had given their blessing. When he got back from battle, the two of them would marry, and when the war was over they'd start a new life, a life that would be so different from the other life he had led.

He feels the light before he actually sees it, but it isn't the bomb he expected. It is the moon emerging out from the cover of cloud. He stares up at the sky and sees the fast wind running, ripping back the cover that hides the glow of the stars. Every man's face turns heavenward. Their collective terror is palpable. If the moon stays clear, they know they'll be picked off like tin ducks in a fall fair shooting gallery.

Guns boom in the eastern sector. Matthew raises his binoculars and scans the water. A convoy of German ships is engaging the landing craft of the third commando, and their boats scatter to the waves like decoys loosed from their tethers. There's no chance of turning back, and any possibility of surprise has been lost with the first rounds of gunfire.

"Jesus, Mary and Joseph," one of the Catholic boys shouts. "We're dead meat now."

Matthew lowers his binoculars and rubs his chest. If only he had known last night what he knows with absolute certainty now: that he will not live to see the day's full light.

"How did you get this one?" Rosie asked, running her index finger along the ropey scar that snaked across his chest.

Matthew recoiled and slapped her hand away so hard

that it bounced off his chest and hit her in the face.

Rosie scrambled away from him and onto her knees. "Why did you do that?" she asked, grabbing up the blankets to cover her breasts.

Matthew swung his legs over the side of the bed and reached for his cigarettes and lighter. There was a dull, hollow clink as he flipped the lighter open. His cupped hands glowed a strange, translucent red in the light of the blue and yellow flame, and his lungs burned as he sucked back the calming rush. He stared at his hands, hands that were big and rough and calloused like his father's.

"I'm sorry," he said, blowing the words out on a funnel of smoke.

They were no sooner out of his mouth than Rosie leaned her body against his and folded him into her arms. He could feel her cheek nestle into the hollow of his shoulder, felt her lips kiss the skin of his neck. "Did somebody hurt you, Matthew? Did somebody cause you this pain?"

Matthew closed his eyes, wrapped his hands around the strength of her forearms and thought about the woman whose round body now enveloped his and what her future would be if he survived. He thought about her tied to a man like his father: a man who lived in the darkness, when what she deserved was a man who stood in the light.

"Your father's wrong about me, Rosie," he said, yanking her arms apart and slapping them aside when she tried to reach out for him again. "It's all been a lie. I've been lying to you right from the start."

Matthew fingers the ring in his pocket and pulls it out. They can't be more than three hundred yards from the beach at Puy, east of the city of Dieppe. Dawn is breaking, and the small chips of sapphire glint in the pale light. Just before she walked out the door, Rosie placed the ring on the bedside table.

"I'm sorry for you," she said, turning back one last time to look at him. "Sorry that you can't let yourself be loved."

Matthew raises his body up just far enough to see over the edge of the boat. The first landing craft hits the beach and is greeted by a great staccato roar. He crouches down, his men poised at the ready, beside and behind him. They lurch forward as the metal box heaves into the sand and sticks. The massive metal door yawns open. He can hear machine gun fire, sees the beach littered with the bodies of the first men in. He smiles broadly, waves his men forward and stands up to welcome death.

And as the bullets spin him back, and his body splashes into the shallow water, he thinks about Rosie, and the words of a poem fall through his memory in a steady rhythm, like the rhythm of light rain, like the gentle wash of the waves that rock his dying body.

CHAPTER 11

1951

Jolene glanced at the order form and stared at the customer in front of her. Charlene was wearing a full shirt-waist dress tonight, midnight blue satin with tiny white dots scattered across the fabric, and she had hard round moonstones clipped to her ears. There was no way she could afford an outfit like that on a secretary's wage. It had to be Eddie footing the bill.

The little shit.

Jolene shoved the order form at her. "How many times have you eaten here, Charlene? You know you need to write the numbers down. The kitchen goes by the numbers, not the names."

Charlene gave her head a little shake and flicked her fingers at the paper in Jolene's hand. "Oh, you can do that. We're right in the middle of something, here. And by the way, has he made our drinks yet?" Charlene asked, pointing a bright red fingernail at Jimmy Chang, who was popping beer bottle caps and mixing cocktails behind the bar. "We ordered them ages ago."

"You ordered them five minutes ago, and no, I don't have time to add the numbers. In case you hadn't noticed, we've got a full house tonight."

"Bitchy never got you a tip, Jolene," Eddie said, peering at her face. "And what's with the shiner? You been walking into doors again?" He leaned back and pointed a finger at her pregnant belly. "Maybe that's making you clumsy. Maybe you should stop work while you're dealing with that."

"And maybe you should have dinner with your wife a little more often, Eddie," Jolene said, tossing their order form back onto the table and throwing a departing glance at Charlene. "Put the numbers down."

Jolene felt Mae Chang's eyes on her as she walked to the bar to pick up her next drink order. Mae didn't like it when Jolene was rude to the customers, but she rarely said anything to her. Instead, Mae would voice her disapproval to her son, Jimmy, and he'd be the one to tell Jolene.

"I'm going to get an earful tonight," Jimmy said, tilting his head in his mother's direction.

Jolene shrugged and double-checked the tray of drinks against her order. "I can't help that," she said. "I'll be damned if I take any more crap off of those two. Eddie's a prick and she's a little gold digger."

"I know that, and you know that, but the only thing my mother knows is that she wanted to fire you two months ago. So I'm the only thing standing between you and the pogey."

"You're a prince among men, Jimmy," Jolene said with a grin as she swept her tray off the counter, extending it in Eddie and Charlene's direction. "Do me a favour? Take their drinks over when they're ready. If I go, I'm liable to slap them silly."

"Sure thing," Jimmy said, reaching for the lemon gin and frowning at the bottle. "Although why people drink this crap is beyond me."

Jolene smiled as she headed down the aisle to the far end of the restaurant. Jimmy Chang was the best friend she had in this hellhole of a town, and the only friend she had at Mae-Mae's Chinese Restaurant.

She was still smiling when she set her tray on the table for four next to the window. "Okay, that's a Black Label for you, Fred, rye and seven for Georgie and a Singapore Sling for Betty. Did I get that right?"

"Right as always, Jolene," Georgie said, taking a swig from his highball glass. "Might as well order me up another one. I'm parched tonight."

Georgie's wife, Betty, rammed her elbow into his ribs, and he laughed. "Okay, okay. No need to get violent," he said and winked at Jolene. "Better scratch that second drink."

Georgie and Betty played out the same scene every Friday night, and Jolene did her best to laugh, on cue, as required.

She glanced over at Fred's wife, Linda. "Sure I can't get you anything?"

"No thanks," Linda said, patting her own pregnant belly. "Doesn't sit right, just now."

Fred put his arm around her. "Can't wait for the big day, can we?"

Linda gave him a small shake of her head and stared at the table. Fred looked confused then glanced at Jolene's huge belly and flushed.

Before he could do something stupid like apologize,

Jolene turned away from the table. "I'll be back with your food order in just a sec."

Jolene walked down the aisle of the restaurant feeling as if every eye in the place was on her: judging her, pitying her. Then she saw Charlene waving her order form in the air like a hankie, and discomfort gave way to a sudden urge for revenge. She walked over and, without a word, plucked the piece of paper out of Charlene's fingers and headed for the kitchen. Instead of posting the order, she shoved it into the pocket of her uniform, grabbed her winter coat, walked straight past the steaming dishes Jimmy's dad was sliding under the heat lamps and banged out the emergency exit at the back.

Pulling on her coat, she brushed a light sprinkling of snow off the wooden crate next to the door. It had snowed for the first time that day, in the early hours of the morning: light feathery drifts that settled over the world like white dust. When she woke, she lay in bed, enjoying the soft, yellow glow of the room, knowing by the quality of light that the snow had finally arrived. It was the first time in months she felt calm, almost safe, cocooned on the pull-out couch in her one room apartment. The loneliness that clung to her like a ghost disappeared, and she was at peace.

Jolene pulled her lighter and cigarettes out of her pocket, lit one and sat down. Stretching out her legs, she stared at the swollen ankles bulging over her white lace-up shoes, then leaned her aching back against the cold brick wall of the restaurant.

Two more months: that was all she had to get through. Just sixty-odd days and everything would return to normal. She would have her life back. She would be alone again. But maybe it was better not to think about that. Better to focus, instead, on getting through the next five hours, waiting on the whims and demands of small-minded small-town takers like Eddie and Charlene.

Jolene took a long drag and stared at the tip of her cigarette, the ember burning into grey ash.

When she was young, the women in town had gossiped about girls like her. "Hard" was the word they used: "She's hard."

Well, if hard was what Jolene had become, then hard was what she'd be. Thirty years old, with bleached blond hair, mouth a slash of bright red lipstick, lashes combed thick with black mascara, and the occasional bruise on her cheek because she didn't take shit from anyone.

Jolene took another drag off her cigarette and struggled to her feet. She walked in a circle, took two more quick puffs and tossed the half-finished cigarette into the snow. As long as she kept moving, the baby kept still, and that suited her just fine. She didn't need a sensory reminder of the life that was growing inside her, a life that no longer belonged to her. It just made her feel guilty and sad, and she didn't like feeling sad. Feeling sad made her want to drink. It made her want to pick up a man.

As if she could pick up a man looking like this.

Jolene pushed back through the door and was pulling off her coat when she spotted Mae Chang at the far end of the kitchen.

"You come fast and take orders now," Mae yelled, pointing at a congealing plate of deep-fried pork balls in sweet and sour sauce. "You are a lazy girl. A lazy, lazy girl."

Jolene extended her left arm and jabbed a finger at the dial of her watch. "I get a fifteen-minute break every night at six fifteen. It's six twenty-five. I only took ten minutes."

"No break when busy. I tell you this. No break when

busy!" Mae balled her hand into a fist and pounded at the air.

Jolene ignored her, piling the plates of lukewarm food onto her serving tray, the air around her oppressive with the smell of boiling fat and Mae's silent fuming. The older woman finally gave up and stomped back into the dining room. As soon as the door swung shut behind her, Mr. Chang turned away from the stove.

"You are not a lazy girl," he said in his carefully phrased English. "But when the food is hot, perhaps it is better to wait for your break."

Jolene shrugged then flashed him a smile as she reached into her pocket and handed him Charlene and Eddie's order. "Take your time with this one," she said.

Mr. Chang grinned back at her. "Someone you do not like?"

"You got that right, Mr. Chang," Jolene said. Pushing her bum against the swinging door, she backed into the dining room then turned around and stopped.

Mae had put that strange Chinese music on the record player again, its odd twanging sound plucking on Jolene's nerves. Mae had lowered the overhead lights as well, so the main source of illumination was now limited to the fake paper lanterns that hung on the edges of the room. Jolene carried her tray through the noisy, darkened restaurant, trying to avoid ramming her hip on a pushed-back chair. As she passed by table sixteen, she heard Hal Wiley's eighty-year-old father, Boyd, start to grumble.

"Who turned off the damn lights?" he said in a voice loud enough for the next five tables to hear. "I can't see my goddamned dinner."

The sound of stifled laughter followed Jolene all the way to Georgie Enfield's table.

"Here we go," she said, setting five dishes down between the foursome. "Beef Chow Mein, Chicken Gai Koo, Sweet and Sour Pork Balls and eight egg rolls. And I asked for some extra rice because of the wait."

She was about to turn away when Fred spoke: "Listen, Jolene, about what I said before."

Betty and Linda were staring at her, their eyes filled with pity.

"Oh, for God's sake, Fred, forget about it." Jolene smiled at the women as if it were all a big joke and slapped her hand against the side of her big belly. "You know me. Skin as thick as leather and just waiting to have it over with. Just give me a shout if there's anything else you need."

As she turned away, she heard a small gasp followed by whispers and Fred's voice saying, "I told you she wouldn't care."

Jolene strode away, swinging the empty tray at her side as if she didn't have a care in the world. She knew she'd shocked the two women, but she didn't give a damn. They were always polite to her, but like everyone else in town, they both thought she was a slut. So what was the difference? Better to play to character.

Better gossip than pity.

She was halfway down the aisle when she noticed a small, lean woman in a flannel shirt, with hair as short as a man's, sitting at a table for one. She had a book in front of her, like she always did, and she was pretending to read, like she always did. The sight of her made Jolene want to run. Instead she took a sharp detour to the left, squeezed past table ten and headed for the bar.

Winnie had been back for a couple of months now, and every Friday night she came into the restaurant, and every Friday night Jolene did her best to ignore her. Winnie was an outsider, an outcast like her, but Jolene knew that two wrongs never did make a right, so she had decided to steer clear of her. Besides, it wouldn't have been fair to encourage her or give her the wrong idea. She'd learned years ago that Winnie didn't need a friend like her. She needed something more. So she spurned Winnie's warmth and easy kindness and kept her distance. She kept herself to herself and as far away from this strange, man-like woman as she could.

Jimmy leaned over the bar. "She walked in five minutes ago," he said in a low voice. "Want me to get Debbie to take her order?"

"Yeah, if you don't mind. I got enough on my hands, with Henry coming in."

"When's he supposed to get here?"

"It's a three-hour drive from the city, so sometime after eight, I guess. But you never know with my brother. He tends to dawdle when he's nervous."

"They've got it all arranged, then?"

"Far as I know," Jolene said. "He's coming down to give me the details."

"Is his wife coming with him this time?"

Jolene laughed. "Are you kidding? Pearl wouldn't give me the time of day. Too bad she wasn't more like her brother."

"Or her sister," Jimmy said, nodding at the shorthaired woman with the book.

Jolene turned around, and Winnie relaxed back into her chair. "Hey, Jolene," she said.

"Oh, hi, Winnie. I didn't see you there."

Winnie eyed her with that newfound confidence of hers, the self-assurance she'd never had as a girl. "You're a lousy liar, Jolene," she said with a laugh and opened her book again.

Jolene found herself standing there, feeling like a child

caught out in a lie by a loving parent. She was about to protest but stopped herself. Better not to engage. Better to ignore her.

She turned to Jimmy and flicked an angry finger at the record player behind the bar. "Put on some Kitty Wells, for Christ's sake. That Chinese stuff is driving me nuts."

By nine o'clock there were only half a dozen customers left, and Jolene was wiping down tables. Eddie and Charlene had left her a pile of pennies as an insult tip, but Charlie and his gang had managed to scrape together a dollar between them, which was pretty good. If she were lucky, she'd make five bucks in tips for the night. Not great but not a bad haul either.

Out of the corner of her eye, she saw Winnie finally get to her feet and pull on her duffel coat. Stuffing her paperback into her jacket pocket, she started toward the door then stopped and turned back.

"You still have that note I left you?" she asked.

Jolene kept her eyes on the table she was cleaning. "I'll see you next Friday, Winnie," she said.

Winnie was almost at the door when the entry bell rang to signal another arrival, and Jolene looked up.

"Shit," she muttered to herself. It was Henry.

"Well, I'll be damned," she heard him shout. "I haven't seen you in years. Well, you can't leave now, Winnie. Come on back and have a drink with me while I wait for Jolene to get off work."

They were making their way toward her, Henry waving and grinning, when the bell dinged again, and Jolene looked up to see Tony and his buddy Al stagger through the door, drunk.

"Hey, you!" Tony shouted at her, his voice booming through the near-empty restaurant. "You done yet? There's a party over at the Dixons'." His friend Al staggered into the table next to the door, almost tipping it over. Tony grabbed his arm, shoved him into a chair then fell into the one beside him.

Jimmy walked out from behind the bar and stood next to Jolene. "You want me to go deal with them?" he asked.

Before she could answer, Henry strolled up. "Hey, Jolene, sorry I'm late. Who're the yahoos at the front?" he asked with a grin, until he got close enough to see the bruise on her face.

"Jolene!" Tony shouted, banging his fists on the table. "Get your ass over here."

The commotion brought Mrs. Chang hurrying out of the kitchen, followed by her husband. She pointed at Jolene. "I told you. No more trouble. No more trouble here."

"I'll deal with it, Mom," Jimmy said. "Just go back and finish the till."

Mae stood her ground, launching into a Mandarin tirade as the restaurant's remaining customers slipped out the door.

"Hey!" Tony shouted, banging on the table again. "You gonna get us a beer, or do I have to come down there and get one myself?"

Winnie turned to Henry. "Maybe we should do something," she said.

Before Henry could answer, Jolene pushed past them. "This is my problem. I'll deal with him."

Winnie grabbed her arm. "And who gave you that?" she asked, pointing at Jolene's bruised eye.

Jolene had never heard her brother yell before, but he

yelled now. "That no-good son of a bitch hit you? Well, let's just see if he can take it as well as he can dish it out."

Henry headed for Tony, with Winnie and Jimmy following close behind. Jolene hesitated then took off after them. She could see Tony eyeing their approach. He leaned his big, muscular body back, lifted his feet onto the table in front of him, crossed his ankles and balanced his weight on the back legs of his chair.

"Pig-boy, a chink and a bull dyke," he said. "Quite the crowd, eh, Al?"

It was Winnie who moved first, locking her foot under the front leg of Tony's chair and yanking up. Jolene watched Tony's arms windmill as he tried to recover his balance, but the chair just kept falling backward until its legs kicked out and Tony crashed to the floor, clipping his head on the edge of the table behind him. He swore, rubbed the back of his skull, and for a split second everything went quiet. There was a sudden roar, and Tony was on his feet again. Grabbing the fallen chair, he turned and heaved it at Winnie, but the chair went wide, hitting a table that had been set for the next day, cracking its surface and scattering water glasses, cutlery and a bottle of China Lily across the linoleum floor. Henry tried moving into the line of fire, but Winnie stood her ground as Tony prepared to charge.

Terrified that he would do to Winnie what he had done to her, Jolene moved to step between them, but Jimmy grabbed her arm. Mae Chang's voice rang out like a siren from the back of the restaurant.

"Police!" she shrieked, waving the receiver of the bar telephone in the air. "You leave now. Police come, right away!"

Al staggered out of his chair and grabbed the sleeve of

Tony's black car coat.

"Come on," he said. "I don't want any trouble. We gotta go before the cops get here."

Tony shook him off and pointed a finger. "I know where you live, Jolene. Just remember that. I can get to you any time I want."

The two men slammed out the door, and Mae Chang rushed at Jolene.

"No more," she said. "You get your coat now. You leave and not come back."

"Come on, Ma," Jimmy said. "She didn't ask them to do this."

Mae cut him off with a wave of her finger, shouting at him in Chinese. Whatever she said made his face turn red and silenced him. He looked away from his mother, turned to Jolene, and she saw in his eyes something she had never seen before – the naked want.

All of her life, men had wanted something from her, taken things from her, and now it was Jimmy, his needs, settling onto her shoulders like a solid, heavy weight. She saw Winnie emerge from the kitchen holding a pale yellow coat in her hands. Winnie, who wanted nothing, demanded nothing. She lifted the coat, spread it open like a pair of wings, and draped it over Jolene's shoulders. Jolene felt a steady arm wrap itself around her and heard Winnie speaking to Henry.

"Let's get her out of here."

Jolene hadn't asked where they were going, had barely registered the disappearance of the street lamps, the headlights eating up the darkness of the road ahead. It was snowing again, gusting into the eye of the windshield.

Jolene blinked as if the icy flakes might blow into her own eyes, then turned away, leaned her head against the door-frame of Winnie's truck and stared into the side-view mirror. She tensed when she saw headlights winking through the snowstorm behind them.

Then she remembered: it had to be Henry.

She heard blinkers clicking as Winnie slowed the truck and turned off to the right, the truck bouncing down a dirt road into an even denser darkness slashed with white. They climbed a rise and a light appeared, glowing from a window.

"Is that your place?" Jolene asked.

"I don't own it yet," Winnie said, pulling the truck to a stop a few feet from a grey two-storey farmhouse. "Looks a bit of a wreck now, but I'll soon have it fixed up."

Winnie jumped out of the truck and was walking toward the passenger side, but Henry got there first. He opened the door and offered Jolene his hand.

She stared at the snowy ground. "I forgot my boots."

"I've got a pair of slippers inside," Winnie said as she made her way toward the house. "I'll get in and put on some coffee."

Henry took Jolene's arm and helped her out of the truck. "I didn't know Winnie was back. When did the two of you become friends?"

"We're not friends," Jolene said as she climbed the stairs that led inside.

Winnie poured coffee out of a silver percolator and handed a cup to Jolene.

She took it, set it on the kitchen table and reached for the cream. "So what's the plan?" she asked.

Henry created a whirlpool in his coffee cup with a spoon. "I think you've had enough for one night. It'll keep till tomorrow."

"Just spit it out, Henry. No sense delaying what needs to be said."

Winnie got up and put the percolator back on the stove to keep it warm. "I can leave, if you want me to," she said.

Jolene shrugged. "Everyone else in town's going to know about it soon enough. You might as well stay." She sipped at her coffee and watched Henry squirm. He finally gave up and stared at his hands.

"Well," he said, "Pearl wanted me to tell you that we've chosen the names. If it's a boy we'll call him Henry Fredrick, after me and our real dad. If it's a girl, Pearl wants to call her Charlene Letitia. She likes the name Charlene, and Lettie was her mother's name."

Jolene stared at her coffee cup. She'd hoped they might choose hers as the second name, but the idea of her child being called Charlene made her stomach turn. She hated the name because she hated the woman, but the child wouldn't be hers, so she had no say.

She glanced at Winnie, saw sympathy in her eyes and immediately looked away. She picked up the sugar bowl and spoke to Henry. "Call it whatever you like," she said. "Where do you want me to stay?"

"We figured on you coming up to the city a week before your due date. Maybe put you up in a motel close to the hospital. We'd have you stay at the apartment," he said, staring down at his coffee cup, "but it's just too small."

Too small for her and Pearl was what he really meant to say.

But when he looked up again, his eyes were so full of love and gratitude that Jolene just had to forgive him.

"Honest to God, Jolene, if we could take you in now, we would. I can't even begin to tell you what this means to us. We've been trying for so long for a baby. Sometimes I think Pearl's half crazy with the wanting of it."

Jolene reached out and covered her brother's hand with her own, wondering how the hell she would keep her own body and soul together until the baby came and she was able to find another job.

"You could always stay here," Winnie said, looking directly at her. "At least until the baby comes and you're on your feet again."

Jolene looked at Henry as if she hadn't even heard Winnie. "We should get back to my place now, get out of Winnie's hair."

Winnie got to her feet. "I don't think that's a good idea. I wouldn't put it past Tony to show up on your doorstep tonight." She walked over to the kitchen window and pushed aside the curtain to peer into the darkness, keeping her back to Jolene. "Besides, the storm is getting worse. Maybe you should both bunk here for the night."

"I don't have my things. I think we should get back."

"Well, I think a bed beats me sleeping on the floor at your place, don't you?" Henry said.

Winnie smiled. "Sorry, Henry, you'll be on the couch tonight. I've only the one spare bed for now. But it's up to Jolene. She needs to be where she's comfortable. So if you're going, Jolene, you'd better get a move on."

Winnie just stood there, staring at her, feet planted on the floor, arms folded loose and easy across her chest, comfortable in her own skin, comfortable with a yes or a no. Daring Jolene to say yes.

"So what do you say?" she asked.

The offer was on the table, and Jolene knew she could

take it or leave it, but the proposition would never be made again. She could be alone, or she could be looked after. She could be loved, no strings attached.

Jolene turned to her brother. "I don't want you to call the child Charlene. I hate the name Charlene."

"Well, hell," Henry said, rubbing the back of his neck. "If you don't like the name, we won't call her that. But what do I tell Pearl? She loves that name."

"What about Darlene?" Winnie asked, walking to stand behind Jolene, reaching out a hand to rest it on her shoulder. "Has the same ring."

Henry thought about it for a minute and nodded. "Pearl just might go for that."

· "Good," Jolene said, getting to her feet. "Now go get your suitcase, Henry. And tomorrow we'll go and fetch my things."

CHAPTER 12

2000

Pearl woke up that morning with a parched throat and a terrible premonition that today was the day she was going to die. She reached for her water glass, but it was empty, as was the carafe on her bedside table.

"Shit," she said as she fumbled around for the call button. It had taken the nurse twenty minutes to get to her room the last time she buzzed the station. If she had been dying that day, she would have been dead ten times over.

Pearl lay back on her pillows, adjusted the horns of the oxygen tube that sat below her nose and wondered how long it would take them this time. She focused her attention on the wall clock opposite the bed, but she still couldn't shake off the nasty feeling that she was about to die. She closed her eyes. She didn't feel sick. She didn't feel any pain. It must be that damned dream she had that was putting these crazy thoughts into her head.

So often Pearl forgot her dreams, but this time, she remembered every detail. She'd been lying in her bed at home, watching her daughters pulling things out of her drawers and tossing them onto the floor as if she were already dead. She couldn't stop them, because she was too weak to move or say anything. They'd been rooting around in her cupboard when Henry showed up, and he and the girls had started to laugh about her as if she wasn't even there. Then the girls suddenly disappeared, and it was just her and Henry in the room. He'd walked over to the bed and stared down at her.

"Your turn now, Pearlie," he said with a smile, but when he reached out and took her hand, she felt so much better that she got right up and started walking around the house. Only it wasn't her house any more. It was the old farmhouse, and Winnie was there, standing in the kitchen, yelling at her to go back upstairs and wait until she called for her. Pearl couldn't understand why her sister was yelling, why she was so frantic to get rid of her. Winnie's body was blocking the door that led to their parents' bedroom, but Pearl could just see past her to the tangle of sheets, the body lying beneath them and a hand, resting, still and open, at the edge of the bed.

"Go back, Pearl!" her sister shouted. "Go back."

But Pearl just stood there, staring at her mother's lifeless hand, and as she did her heart beat faster and faster, and a huge wind blew open the door, covering the floor in drifts of dust and tumbling balls of Russian thistle. She looked around the room. Every window was smashed in, and when she looked up all she could see was blue sky and sunlight through a huge hole in the roof. Then everything went black, she heard a loud creaking sound, and the wind came up again. The dust whirled up off the floor and spun around her like a dervish, its fine grey silt blinding her, filling her open mouth and closing off her throat. She was being buried alive, buried like her mother. She started to run, but she couldn't breathe, she couldn't see, and she couldn't remember where the door was.

She woke up, gasping for air, pushing back the rough hospital sheets as if they were a heavy layer of dirt.

"You rang, Mrs. Calder?"

Pearl opened her eyes, and that nice young nurse, the one she liked, was standing at the end of her bed. Colleen, her name was, a pretty little thing with a powder blue uniform and gentle hands.

Pearl managed a smile as Colleen flipped on the overhead light. "Sorry for the trouble," she said. "But I'm out of water."

Colleen walked over, picked up the carafe and headed toward the bathroom. "You're up early," she said. "How are you feeling?"

"A bit off," Pearl called out over the sound of the running water. "But nothing too serious."

Colleen walked out of the bathroom and smiled. "Expecting anyone today?"

"I suppose my daughters'll be up at some point. Maybe a few friends."

"You're a lucky woman, Mrs. Calder," Colleen said as she poured a glass of water and handed it to Pearl.

"Oh?" Pearl said, reaching for the glass. "And why's that?"

"You get so many visitors," Coleen said with a wink. "People must really love you."

Pearl frowned at her water.

"I'll be back with your meds at seven thirty. Light on or off?" Colleen asked as she passed the switch.

"Turn it off. Maybe I'll sleep a bit."

But Pearl knew that she wasn't going to sleep. She just

wanted to sit in the dark and think. That bloody dream was all Darlene's fault, really, her fault and Henry's. If he'd thrown those things out like she'd told him to, Darlene wouldn't be in here every second day pestering her with questions, and she wouldn't be lying in this goddamned hospital bed, dreaming about things she didn't want to remember. Bad enough she was burdened with it. She had decided years ago that she wasn't going to burden her kids.

"But why didn't you tell us about your family?" Darlene had asked. "Don't you see what a difference it might have made?"

"What was there to tell? My parents died the same year and Matthew died a few years later in the war. Winnie ran off when I was fifteen. I didn't see her again until long after I was married."

"But why, Mom? Dad went out to see them. Why didn't you? Why didn't you go out to see your own sister? Were you ashamed of her?"

Pearl caught hold of the sheet with one hand and slammed her fist down on the bed with the other. "What went on between my sister and me had nothing to do with that. Nothing!"

She opened her mouth, trying to fill her empty lungs, and Darlene rushed to the side of the bed. "Oh God, Mom, I'm so sorry. I didn't mean to upset you."

Pearl waved her away with a sharp motion of her hand. "I'm not bloody well upset, Darlene. I'm fed up. And I don't want to talk about this again."

Pearl set her water glass on the bedside table, lay back on her pillows and stared at the ceiling. Was it so wrong not to have told her kids? And even if she told them now, what would she say? How could she explain it all, when she didn't even understand it herself?

Maybe it would be just as well if she did kick the bucket. At least then there would be no more questions.

Pearl turned onto her side and stared out the window. The room was bathed in the grey dust of twilight, but the cotton blind was the soft yellow white of the rising sun. Pearl closed her eyes against the dawn and thought about her daughters. So many things left unsaid and so many secrets, particularly when it came to Darlene.

And then there was Carol. The child who had been so much like Mattie: the dreamy one, the one who had spent her childhood with her brain floating up in a cloud somewhere. Pearl felt as if she had spent the first fifteen years of Carol's life grabbing at her ankles, trying to pull her feet back down to earth. But no matter how hard she tried, Carol kept floating away on all those big dreams of hers, and when she finally fell, she hit the ground with such a God almighty crash that it had changed everything, changed her beyond all recognition.

And maybe Carol had been right to blame her. Maybe it had been her fault. Maybe she had always expected too much.

Pearl flipped over onto her back a little too quickly, and the room pitched and heaved. She pressed her palms against the mattress and lay as still as she could, waiting for the bed to stop rocking and the floor to right itself. Maybe her blood pressure was spiking again. There were black spots bursting at the centre of her eyes, and her heart was pounding like a hammer. Maybe she was dying.

Pearl pressed her hands into the mattress, waiting for her heart rate to slow, and thought about Henry. How he'd been little more than a bag of bones when he died. How brave he'd been and how she'd sat there, day after day, watching him die, unable to speak, unable to tell him, sure there would be more time.

Pearl took a deep breath and let it out slowly. She closed her eyes and started to drift. There was always so little time. There was always so goddamned little time.

At eleven o'clock that morning, she was sleeping in a warm pool of sunlight when her friends arrived: Jean hidden behind a pot of yellow mums, Izzie loaded down with a box full of food.

"This is for you," she said, setting the box on the bed and lifting the lid. "We thought you might need a change."

Pearl reached in and pulled out a plate of fancy sandwiches, a tin of muffins and a little tray of mixed squares. "Thank God," she said, staring at the rows of cherry slice and matrimonial cake. "Go on down to the nurses' station and tell Colleen to put the coffee on. They've got one of those drip machines behind the desk."

Izzie headed for the door, and Pearl called out after her: "And tell her to come on down and eat something. There's enough food here to feed an army."

Jean cleared a space on the bedside table for the mums.

"I always did love yellow," Pearl said, reaching out to touch a blossom. "Like having the sun right here next to me."

"That's just what I thought," Jean said, reaching out to pat Pearl's hand. "How are you feeling?"

"Like I could die happy," Pearl said as she popped a tuna and cream cheese pinwheel sandwich into her mouth and crunched down on the gherkin in the middle.

"Izzie and I figured you wouldn't want to be alone today. We thought a little party might be in order."

Pearl frowned and looked up at her friend. "A party? What the devil for, Jean?" she asked, her mouth still full of tuna and sweet pickle.

"Don't you remember? It's your wedding anniversary today."

Pearl tried to swallow, but the sandwich had lodged in her throat. "Oh Jesus," she said when she finally pushed it down. "I lost track of the time."

"July 19, and just as bright and sunny then as it is today," Jean said and sighed. "My mother warned me when Charlie died. The special days are always the hardest."

Pearl didn't answer. She just stared out the hospital window, then leaned back on the pillows and closed her eyes.

Pearl had spent her first anniversary working in the Notions Department at the Woolworth's store. She had been busy re-stocking the button shelves and was five minutes away from her morning coffee break, when someone tapped her on the shoulder.

"Excuse me, miss, but isn't twenty-five cents just a bit pricey for a zipper?"

Pearl stiffened as she set a handful of cardboard-backed buttons onto the counter in front of her. She was constantly dealing with complaints like this one, usually from cheap old ladies who thought that nothing should ever go up in price. She turned around, poised to do battle, and was greeted by a smile.

"Oh my God! " she shouted, throwing her arms around Jean and hugging her. "What the hell are you doing here?

Why didn't you tell me you were coming into town?"

"I wanted to surprise you," Jean said, hugging her back. "Happy anniversary, Pearl."

Pearl gestured at the endless rows of needles and thread and laughed. "Some anniversary. I'm stuck here, and Henry won't even remember."

"Oh, I wouldn't be too sure about that," Jean said as she slid her arm into Pearl's. "How about a coffee? Can you take your break?"

Pearl nodded. "I'll meet you at the lunch counter in five minutes. Go and save us a seat."

She watched as Jean walked down the aisle. She was wearing a new print dress with tiny daisies on it, and her hat was white with a matching daisy trim. Pearl stared down at the black pumps she'd had re-heeled for the umpteenth time and the skirt she'd just re-hemmed in an effort to make it a bit more stylish. Jean's husband, Charlie, was a bank clerk, and he must have been doing well to afford an outfit like the one Jean had on. Unlike Henry, the grease monkey, who couldn't even earn enough money for her to quit work and finally get pregnant, let alone buy a new summer outfit.

It had been the same thing at their weddings, the summer before. Jean's mother had hired a woman to make Jean a real bridal gown, white satin, with long, full sleeves and a bias-cut train that pooled around her feet like water. While Pearl bought six yards of dove grey crepe and sewed herself a suit, instead of a wedding gown, because she knew she'd be able to wear it again.

"Imagine. Grey instead of white on your wedding day," her aunt Clara had said in disgust. "People are going to think you gave it away. And no doubt they'd be right."

Pearl had intended to say that white was an impractical

colour, that it soiled easily and was no good after Labour Day, whereas her beautiful, dove grey suit with its sleeveless tunic, below-the-knee skirt and long jacket could be worn at any time of the year. Instead, she had yelled at her aunt, "I don't give a good goddamn what other people think, least of all you. You're not paying for this wedding. In fact, you're not even invited."

Pearl shoved the rest of the buttons into their narrow wooden display case. She'd been happy as a clam not to have her aunt and uncle at the wedding, and she didn't give two hoots that she'd had no reception. She'd just been glad to get it over with.

Pearl headed for the soda counter. She had said yes to marrying Henry because she was afraid that no one else would ask. Oh, she liked him well enough, that was true, but she felt no great passion for him. She'd had a passion for Joe Walker, and she firmly believed that you only got one shot at something like that.

Pearl scanned the soda counter and spotted Jean sitting at the far end. She took the seat next to her and waved at the waitress. Gertie strode down the aisle with a cup and saucer in one hand and a coffee pot in the other.

"The usual?" she asked as she splashed coffee into the cup.

Pearl scanned the display case above the sandwich counter. "No, I think I'll have the banana cream today. How about you, Jean? Would you like some pie?"

Jean's hand flitted over her coffee cup. "Oh no. Coffee's just fine."

"How about a refill, then?" Gertie asked. "It's on the house."

Jean's face flushed as she swallowed the dregs of her coffee and set her cup down a little too quickly. It rattled and rocked against the saucer, and her hands fluttered around it like two nervous birds.

Gertie laughed as she steadied the cup and filled it to the brim. "Then again, maybe you've had enough," she said and turned away to cut a slice of pie.

Once she was out of earshot, Pearl arched a brow at Jean. "Don't tell me you're on a diet. I'm the one who should be dieting, not you."

Jean stared at her cup. "No. Just a little short on money, that's all."

"Who isn't?" Pearl sighed as she shook some sugar into her coffee and stirred it in.

"Well, never mind that," Jean said with forced cheeriness. "How about we drive out to the Half Moon for some hotdogs and beer tonight? Just the four of us. It won't cost much, and I don't know about you, but I could use a good time."

Pearl just stared at her. "Are you all right, Jean?" she asked.

Jean turned back to her coffee. "Of course I'm all right. So what do you say? Are you up for some fun?"

"Sounds like a grand idea," Pearl said as she sipped at her coffee, wondering what was troubling her friend.

She didn't have to wait long to find out. When she walked in the door of her Ellice Street apartment after work, Jean and Charlie were already there. Henry greeted her at the door and pulled her into the kitchen, where he promptly kissed her, wished her a happy anniversary and informed her that Charlie was on his fifth rye and seven.

"I don't think he should be driving us anywhere," he said. "We likely wouldn't get there in one piece."

But when they walked into the living room to suggest that Pearl make dinner at home, Charlie wasn't having any of it. "I'm fine," he said, lurching to his feet. His drink sloshed over the edge of his glass and spattered across the floor, but Charlie didn't seem to notice. Pearl glanced over at Jean, who had shrunk a little further into her chair.

"Okay, Charlie," Henry said. "You just sit yourself down. We're not going anywhere. I've got an anniversary gift for Pearl, and she hasn't opened it yet."

"And I'm not leaving this apartment until I get a cup of coffee," Pearl chimed in. She winked at Jean, who smiled with relief. Then she turned to follow Henry back down the narrow hall to the kitchen.

Henry handed her the coffee tin. "I lied, Pearl. I didn't know what else to say to stop him, but I don't have a gift," he said, reaching into his back pocket and handing her a wrinkled envelope. "Just a card."

Pearl took the envelope, tossed it onto the kitchen table and reached for the coffee percolator. Henry cast a sorrowful look at the abandoned card.

Pearl threw up her hands. "Oh, for Christ's sake, Henry, don't start. I'll open it later. Right now I just need to get some coffee down that damn fool's throat."

Charlie had been more or less sober by the time they got to the Half Moon restaurant, but two hot dogs and five beers later he was slurring his words again. When they finished eating, the three of them half carried, half dragged him to the car and heaved him into the back. They were about to slam the door shut when Charlie lunged across the seat, pitched his head and his hotdogs over the side and passed out. They pushed his dead weight back in, and

Jean cried as she wiped his open mouth with a hankie. Pearl got into the front seat, and Henry started the car.

They were winding their way down the road that ran past the river when Jean finally spoke. "The bank fired him. He can't find another job."

"Oh, Jesus," Pearl said, reaching her hand over the seat and patting her friend's knee. "If there's anything we can do, Jean…"

Jean shook her head, and they drove the rest of the way in silence.

When they reached the outskirts of the city, Pearl turned to look at Henry. His eyes were focused on the road, and his hardened, grease-stained hands, hands that he scrubbed every day after work but could never get fully clean, rested easily on the wheel. And as she watched her husband drive, Pearl realized that for the first time in her life, she felt completely safe. So she closed her eyes, leaned her head against Henry's shoulder and fell sound asleep.

"Are you tired, Pearl?" Jean asked.

"Just a bit of a headache," Pearl said, opening her eyes. "I'll rest for a few more minutes, if you don't mind. You and Izzie just sit and chat."

Pearl closed her eyes, and the voices of her two friends floated around her like a comforting song.

Jean and Charlie had moved into the city shortly after the hot dog fiasco, and over the next ten years, Charlie drank his way through half a dozen jobs then died of a heart attack at the age of forty-two. By that time, Pearl didn't have much use for him, but she still felt sad, not just for Jean but for Charlie, because he wouldn't live to see his kids grow up, would never hold his grandchildren, would never be able to mend his ways.

The thought chilled her, so she turned onto her side, gripped the stiff, bleached hospital sheet in both hands and pulled it up to her chin.

When Pearl surfaced again, she could hear voices, but they didn't belong to Izzie and Jean. She peered through her eyelashes and saw Carol and Darlene sitting in the chairs at the end of the bed. She wasn't ready to talk to either one of them, so she closed her eyes and drifted again. The next time she awoke, the room felt empty, but she found a young woman leaning against the end of the bed. She was staring out the window, her hands laced across her belly, the afternoon sun playing in her short black hair.

She looked so much like Winnie that the sight of her left Pearl breathless. She took in a deep gasp of air then coughed so hard she had to sit up to clear her throat. Darlene's girl-friend, Athena, raced down the length of the bed and started pounding on her back. Pearl waved her arms to signal that she'd had enough, took a deep breath and pointed a finger in the general direction of Athena's abdomen.

"I don't particularly want to know how you managed that," she said, "but just how far along are you?"

Athena stared at her stomach then looked up. "Twelve weeks. How did you know?"

"The way you were standing," Pearl said, reaching for her water glass and taking a sip. "It's a girl, you know. You're carrying low and wide like I did with Carol. The boys tend to ride up high and blow your belly out."

"You're right. It is a girl."

"What are you going to call her?"

"I thought maybe Lillian Pearl."

Pearl snorted. "And what does Miss Darlene think about that?"

"I don't really know," Athena said, staring at the floor. "I'm not really living there any more."

"And why the hell not?"

Athena shrugged. "I don't think she wants this baby."

"Oh, for Christ's sake. Nobody knows if they want a baby. You just do it."

"It's a bit more complicated than that."

Pearl shook her head. "It's always complicated when it comes to Darlene. She thinks too much. Always has. I don't know where the hell she gets it from. Certainly not her father's family, that's for damn sure."

Athena smiled sadly. "You must miss him a lot."

She was tempted to say that how she felt about Henry was her business, but Athena looked so bereft that Pearl thought better of it.

"Yes," she said. "Strangely enough, I do."

"My mother died when I was eighteen, and I still miss her. Now more than ever, I think."

Pearl stared at her empty hands. "Getting pregnant will do that." She looked up to find Athena staring at her. The young woman's face was still, her eyes as black as Winnie's.

"You were an orphan, weren't you?" Athena said. "It must have been hard not knowing your mother."

Pearl opened her mouth to speak and found that she couldn't, so she closed her eyes against the rush of sadness, the ancient grief. How could a little bit of sympathy do this? How could sympathy make you feel as if your heart had just been torn in two?

"Are you all right, Mrs. Calder?"

Pearl opened her eyes and stared at the small dark-haired woman who stood at the edge of her bed. There was a calmness in her, an otherworldliness, like staring into the cool, dark eyes of a ghost. It would be so easy to tell her: a way to atone for the past, a way to make amends with a future she would likely never see.

Pearl leaned back on her pillows and closed her eyes. "I'm going to tell you something," she said. "And when I'm gone, I want you to tell my kids."

CHAPTER 13

1954

Pearl waited while Henry put their overnight bag into the trunk of the car and slammed it shut. He walked around to the passenger door and unlocked it. Pearl lifted one foot onto the runner board, put her hand onto the back of the seat to steady herself and angled her pregnant belly through the doorframe.

"Are you sure she'll be all right?" Henry asked once she'd settled. "I don't like the idea of leaving her alone."

"Oh, for God's sake, Henry, quit wringing your hands. Darlene's not alone, she's with Jean and Charlie. And besides, we're only gone till tomorrow afternoon."

Henry shook his head. "I don't know why we're not bringing her. I know they'd love to see her again."

Pearl folded her arms across her ample breasts and stared at the windshield. Henry gave up, closed the door and walked around to the driver's side. He got in and patted Pearl's stomach. "How's he doing?"

"I told you, Henry. It's not a boy. It's a girl. Now get your hand off me and drive. The sooner we get there, the sooner we get home."

Henry sighed, slid the key into the ignition and pulled away.

Twenty minutes later, they reached the outskirts of the city. Pearl clasped her hands over her belly and settled back to try to nap. It was a miracle, really, this pregnancy. After two miscarriages and one stillborn child, she and Henry had finally welcomed Darlene into their lives and then all but given up hope on the idea of having their own child. A few weeks before Darlene's third birthday, Pearl realized that two months had passed since her last period. When another month passed, she had finally allowed herself to hope. It wasn't until she was well into her fourth month that she actually went to the doctor and had her hopes confirmed.

"What did I tell you?" the doctor had said, slapping his thigh and grinning. "You adopt a child, you quit worrying and bingo. Hubby gets you pregnant."

Pearl had bristled at the idea of sex with Henry being described as something akin to a bingo game, but she'd been so happy that she'd kept her mouth shut and her thoughts to herself. Besides, she wasn't out of the woods yet, and she needed to keep this know-it-all doctor on her side.

Now she was free and clear, she was sure of it, because it was month eight and she could still feel her daughter jostling around, her movements growing stronger and stronger with each passing day, as if she were just raring to get out and see the world. Unlike her baby boy, who had stopped moving in the sixth month and been born dead three months later.

"We don't know why these things happen, but there's no reason to believe it will happen again," the doctor had said as if death were a physical thing, like a car or an airplane that had unexpectedly whisked her boy away.

Pearl sighed and closed her eyes. Better not to think about that now. Better to focus, instead, on the beginning of a new life rather than a sad and sorrowful end. There would be time enough for that once they got to where they were going.

Twenty miles outside Brandon, Henry pulled over at a roadside rest stop: just two picnic tables under a couple of birch trees, and all around them nothing but flat land and ripening grain as far as the eye could see. Pearl pulled the collar of her maternity top away from her chest and blew down her blouse to try to dry off the sweat that was beading along her collarbones and running down her breasts. Then she lifted the loose-fitting blouse and shook it out like a dust rag to cool her damp belly.

"Your ankles are swelling," Henry said, pointing at her feet before pulling the basket of sandwiches and coffee out of the backseat. "You should ride back here the rest of the way and keep your feet up."

Pearl harrumphed. "If I'm back there, I won't be able to tell you how to drive, now, will I?"

Henry laughed as he angled his long legs under the picnic table, set the basket down, opened it and handed her one of the Klik and mustard sandwiches she'd carefully folded into envelopes of waxed paper the night before. Pearl sat down on the opposite bench, stomach out, back to Henry, looking out across a golden sea to the blessed sight of an endless horizon. She had been tense and fidgety for the last ten miles, lifting her foot for an imaginary brake pedal every time Henry got too close to another vehicle, flailing her hands at the dashboard every time he pulled out to pass a farmer dawdling along the highway in a tractor. The baby had been equally active, kicking against Pearl's stomach as if sensing her mother's anxiety. Now she could feel the child's motion slow and her own shoulders unwind as she stared at the horizon. At long last, she was able to fully breathe, pulling in deep gusts of fresh air like a claustrophobic released from a narrow, moving closet.

Pearl leaned her back against the rough edge of the picnic table and took a bite of her sandwich. She thought about the city that way too: like a huge dark closet or a canyon surrounded by buildings instead of mountains. Sometimes she thought she'd go crazy, like the day she'd been shopping downtown with Darlene. She had walked out of Eaton's department store and the surrounding buildings loomed over her like great limestone and brick giants. So she folded up the stroller, hoisted Darlene onto her hip and got onto a bus, riding it to the end of the line, to the edge of the city, where she could see the horizon again.

Pearl shook her head and bit down on her sandwich. It had been a damned silly thing to do, despite the temporary relief it brought, because it had taken her the better part of an hour to get home. Darlene, diaper full, stomach empty, had been screaming bloody murder by the time they got there.

Pearl turned around to find Henry watching her. "Are you worried about seeing her again?" he asked.

"Why should I be worried?" Pearl popped the rest of her sandwich into her mouth and crushed its waxed paper wrapper into a ball. "It's not like I've never seen anyone who's dying before."

She got up, tossed the paper ball into the picnic basket and headed back toward the car. When she got to the door, she turned around, expecting Henry to be there to unlock it for her, and instead found him standing where she'd left him, next to the picnic table, staring at her as if he'd never seen her before.

Ten miles later, they turned south and drove through a landscape flat as a becalmed sea, a sea with little islands of trees cutting through it. She remembered one such island that ran the length between her father's two fields, a windbreak that held the soil down and protected what little grain had grown on either side. But in the years when the rains never came, and the grasshoppers crunched underfoot like dead leaves, even the trees couldn't hold the soil to the earth, and it had filled the air like a dense grey cloud ascending into the skies of hell. She remembered the year she was seven, walking to the school bus day after day with a damp handkerchief tied across her nose and chin, wondering if there would ever be a time when she could pull on a dress or crawl under sheets that didn't feel as if they had been woven from sandpaper.

Now the fields that stretched out on either side of the car were full, and the whiskered grain that flashed by the window in smudges of green and yellow and gold stood tall, heads fat with seed, plump with the rain that had come, as every farmer begged for it to come, at just the right time.

The strange mixture of pleasure and sadness she felt when looking at the fields made her want to laugh and cry, so she yanked her maternity top down to straighten it, folded her arms and focused her eyes on the road ahead.

This was just damned silliness, sitting here feeling sorry for herself like a whiny child. She was a grown-up woman now. She had her own life, her own family, and everything and everyone else was dead and gone, or at least soon would be.

"Just a few more miles," Henry said, pointing at a road sign that zipped by too fast for her to read. "Maybe we should stop in town and pick up a few things. I'd just about kill for a cold drink right about now."

"So would I," Pearl said, pushing her short, permed bangs off her sweaty forehead. "Although it may not be hot for long."

Pearl watched as Henry's eyes followed her finger to the horizon, where a thunderhead hung like a mound of charcoal batting in an otherwise clear blue sky. It looked as if a giant hand had reached under its base, ripping out the rain in long, stretched wisps of grey cotton that floated down from cloud to the earth.

"There's a storm on the Saskatchewan side," she said. "Maybe we'll get it tonight."

It was two in the afternoon when they stopped at a grocery store on First Street. They bought some eggs and bacon for the morning and a carton of soft drinks, two for now, four to share in the evening. Pearl was sucking up the dregs of an Orange Crush through a paper straw when they passed the road that led to the old farmstead.

"Do you want to drive down and say hello?" Henry asked.

"Not on your life." Pearl dropped her empty soda bottle onto the floor. "It'll be a frosty Friday in hell before I say two words to that man."

Pearl's cousin Eddie had done what they all figured he'd do: made a hash of everything. Couldn't farm worth a damn, so he now lived in the old farmhouse that had once belonged to Pearl's father, rented out the land to the neighbours and worked in town at the John Deere, selling combines and tractors to other men, who knew what they were about. According to Henry, Winnie had offered to buy the farm back, a little bit at a time, but Aunt Clara and Uncle Edward would have none of that, so Winnie had bought a house and an acre of land just two miles down the road. A year later, Clara, the old battle-axe, dropped dead and six months after that Edward followed her.

When Henry came home with the news of her aunt and uncle's demise, Pearl had done a little jig in the kitchen of their Hull Street apartment.

"More to be pitied than scorned," Henry said, shaking his head at Pearl's antics.

"Oh, shut up, Henry," Pearl had snapped. "You didn't live with them."

And he hadn't been left alone with them either, not as she had been left when Winnie had walked out on her and hitched a ride to the big city of Winnipeg.

Winnie had returned to the country just shortly after Pearl and Henry had loaded up their borrowed truck and driven all of their worldly goods to the city she had just left. At the time, Winnie had no idea that she was married or that she was moving away, because Pearl had never re-sponded to any of her sister's letters. The first year, she'd tossed Winnie's letters into a box, unopened and unread. Even when curiosity got the better of her, she never wrote back, never called or spoke to her sister. As far as she was concerned, Winnie had betrayed and abandoned her, leav-ing her to fend for herself in a house where no one wanted her and no one loved her, and there was no forgiving that.

"She's dying, Pearl," Henry had said to her. "Jolene says she doesn't have much more than a year. Maybe less."

And that was when the war had escalated, the war Pearl waged between what she said and what she sometimes felt. What she had felt that day was panic, a fear that sliced through her like a cold, sharp gutting knife. But the pain had lasted no longer than a single breath, the wound instantly dressed and healed by an older, more familiar emotion.

"She's been dead to me these past ten years," she replied, picking up the dishrag from the kitchen sink and scouring the counter. "This just makes it official."

Henry had walked up behind her and put his arms around her shoulders. "You don't mean that," he whispered into her ear.

Pearl had wanted to lean her head back against the side of his neck, stand there enfolded in his arms, feeling the warmth of his body against her back, the strength of his arms across her upper chest. Instead, she pulled away from him and went back to cleaning the kitchen.

But over the next few weeks, Henry had slowly worn her down, stroking and nudging, convincing her to go back home and see her dying sister.

Henry slowed the car, and a dirt road appeared on their right. As he turned the corner, Pearl read the names printed in bright red paint on the metal mailbox that sat at the side of the road: *Calder and McKay.*

According to Henry, Winnie had saved his sister's life. She'd been drinking hard and throwing herself at any man who'd buy her a beer, so she'd lost her job in town waiting tables at the Chinese restaurant. Winnie had offered her a place to stay, and Jolene had never left.

Pearl could see why. As the car crested a short rise, a house appeared at the end of the road. It was a plain two-storey clapboard affair with a small, sloping veranda, but it had a smooth coat of chalk-white paint and the same bright red trim she'd seen on the mailbox. A tangle of flowerbeds hugged the walls on either side of the porch, broad beds filled with lilac and peony bushes, great puffs of baby's breath, green whips of daylilies, the high, dead stalks of delphiniums, and in front of them, huge mounds of black-eyed Susans. Beyond the house stood a grey-timbered barn with a sagging roof that listed so far to the left it looked as if it might fall over. Beside it was a vegetable patch enclosed in a seven-foot chicken wire fence to keep out the deer. It was having less success with the crows, which were swooping down to feed on the ripening corn.

Pearl looked back at the house and saw someone sitting on the porch. The figure stood and waved as Henry wheeled to a full stop. The billowing dust that had followed behind the car suddenly caught up with them, fogging the windows with a fine layer of powdery earth that filtered through the cracks, settling on Pearl's hands, the pleats of her skirt, the tops of her flat leather loafers. Fear gripped her, and she stamped her feet to loosen the grit while Henry hopped out of the car to open the door for her. By the time she got out, Jolene was standing beside them. She was carrying a white purse with a cracked leather handle and wearing a sleeveless powder-blue blouse and a dirndl skirt made of yellow cotton that billowed around her thin, stringy legs like a balloon. She hugged Henry, glanced through the back window of the car at the empty seat then eyed Pearl with a mixture of anger and defiance.

"So you finally made it out," she said, then turned back to talk to Henry. "She's had a bad morning, so she's still in bed. There's coffee and stew on the stove and a couple of beers in the fridge. I thought I'd go into town. Give you time to visit."

"Will you be back for dinner?" Henry asked.

"I'm not sure," Jolene said as she opened the door of the truck next to them. She got in, slammed the door shut and rolled down the window. "Eat when you want. I'll be back when I'm back."

Pearl stared at Jolene as she backed up and drove away. Then she lifted her nose and snorted. "Well, that was quite the howdy-do," she said and started toward the house. "Get the bags, Henry. I'm going inside."

She got as far as the veranda door before she realized what she was about to do. She wanted to turn around, tell Henry to start the car up again and drive back to the city. She was staring through the screen of the veranda, contemplating how she might escape, when a ghost appeared and stood in the open doorway of the house.

Suddenly, Pearl was ten years old again. She was standing in the kitchen, and Winnie was telling her what to do.

"You have to go in," she heard her sister say. "You have to say goodbye to Mom before we leave for school."

"But I don't want to go," Pearl said as she ran toward the screen door. "It smells in there."

The rasping click of a door latch, the sound of someone's voice, and Pearl looked up.

"Well? Are you coming in?" Winnie asked.

The woman who stood before her looked nothing like the sister she remembered. Once stocky and square, the plumpness of Winnie's body had been eaten away by the cancer, revealing big, angular bones so strange in someone of such small stature. Her hair was short and razor cut and her skin, once pink and olive, was as drawn and sallow as an old woman's, her bloated stomach almost as big as Pearl's. She seemed to be barely standing, teetering on air as if her feet couldn't quite grip the earth.

"My God," Pearl said. "You look like Mom."

Winnie smiled and started toward her, but Pearl stepped back, reaching for the porch railing with one hand, pressing the other against her pregnant stomach.

"You should be in bed," she said.

Winnie sighed. "I'm sick to death of bed. I'd rather be up and around." She turned, pushed through the screen door, held it open for her sister and waited.

It was dark beyond the doorway, the interior of the house hidden from view. Pearl pushed herself off the railing, forced herself to move forward, through the open door and into the hallway.

The scene that greeted her brought her to a full stop. Stacks of newspaper were lined up against the wall in three-foot piles, narrowing the passageway to a two-foot squeeze, and up the staircase, on every single step, were smaller stacks of magazines – *True Confessions, Star Weekly, Movie Screen*. Pearl stared through the open door of the coat closet and was greeted by a similar scene: balls of string, folded sheets of brown paper and cardboard boxes piled up to the hems of the coats.

She could feel Winnie behind her. "Jolene likes to save things," she said.

Pearl shook her head. "Pray God nobody strikes a match," she said and headed down the hallway.

The kitchen was in somewhat better shape, but still in desperate need of a good clean. *Something to do*, Pearl thought and opened the broom closet door. Taking down the apron she found hanging inside, she tied it around her stomach as best she could and walked to the stove. She lifted the lid of the pot that sat on one of the burners and stared at the grey, congealed mass Jolene had described as stew.

"Nobody's eating this crap," she said, grabbing the pot and dumping its contents into a garbage pail. She strode over to the fridge, where she found a lone package of ground beef wrapped tight in butcher's paper.

"Meat loaf or Swiss steak?" she asked, turning toward her sister.

Winnie smiled as she eased her wasted body into a chair. "Make what you like. I don't eat much these days."

"You need to keep your strength up." Pearl turned back to the counter and stopped. The baby was kicking again, thrusting what felt like a foot against the top of her stomach, pushing into her ribcage. Pearl lifted her fingers to the bulge of foot or hand and rubbed it tenderly.

"Is the baby moving?" Winnie asked. "Can I touch it?"

Pearl hesitated for a second too long, and Henry came striding into the kitchen.

"I put the bag upstairs," he said, turning to Winnie. "How about I get at that garden of yours? It looks like it could use a bit of a harvest."

"Thanks, Henry." Winnie nodded. "That'd be nice."

Pearl had wanted to tell him to stay, to stand between them as a buffer, but he was out the door and gone before she could open her mouth. She looked at Winnie. Her sister's eyes were closed, her head resting against the back of her chair. Her skin was grey, her breathing shallow and short.

The baby was doing somersaults now, turning round and round, sloshing back and forth in the tiny sea of her stomach. Pearl held her belly, feeling her little girl dive and roll as she stood and watched the still, sleeping face of the stranger who was her sister.

How had she allowed this to happen?

Winnie moaned in her sleep, and Pearl strode over to her chair. "That's it," she said, reaching out her arm. "You're going back upstairs whether you want to or not."

Winnie's eyes opened, and she reached out her arms like a child asking to be carried. Pearl slid her own big arms around her sister, lifted her from the chair and helped her upstairs.

The second floor was hot as a cook-stove, and all she could find in her sister's bedroom was one small fan. Pearl aimed it at Winnie, who was dozing in a chair by the window. She crossed the tiny hallway to start a bath, leaving the water running while she returned to make up her sister's bed. She stripped the sour-smelling sheets off the mattress and hunted down the linen closet, where she found a clean flannel pair. After hurrying back to the bedroom, she tossed the sheets on the bed, walked to the window and unclipped the screen. Grabbing the coverlet, she flung it out the window and shook it out into the fresh air. When she finished making the bed, she helped Winnie to the bathroom, turning off the taps and watching as her sister struggled with the clip on her jeans, too weak to get it open. Without a word, she lifted Winnie's arms and pulled off her loose-fitting shirt, undid her pants, and pulled them down. Her body smelled as sour as the sheets, and as her pants fell to the floor, Pearl swallowed the howl building at the back of her throat.

She was still so young, but there was nothing left of her. Nothing left.

"Doesn't that woman ever help you with a bath?" she asked, picking up the jeans and slamming them into the hamper.

"Of course she does," Winnie said, steadying her hands on either side of the tub, slowly lowering herself down. "But it scares her, Pearl. It scares her to see me like this."

"That's no excuse," Pearl said. "She's a grown-up woman, not a child."

Winnie's eyes stared up at her with such kindness and empathy that Pearl looked away.

"I'll get you a face cloth," she said.

Winnie pointed at the door. "The closet's out there."

By the time she returned, Winnie had managed to slide down the back of the old claw-foot tub, immersing her body in the warm, still water. Pearl handed her the face cloth, and Winnie lifted a weary hand, her eyes dulled even by this small exertion. Pearl stared at her for just a moment, then reached for the soap, put her own hands on the side of the tub, and kneeled down. Tucking her big pregnant belly under the rim, she took hold of her sister's arm and gently began to scrub.

When Winnie could stand no more, Pearl helped her out of the bath and into a clean pair of pajamas. She led her back to the bedroom, and Winnie sat on the side of the bed, hands gripping the edge of the mattress, her eyes fixed on the floor.

"What do you have for the pain?" Pearl asked.

Winnie pointed at a bottle on the dresser. "But they knock me out. I can't think straight."

"Never mind that. I'll still be here when you wake up." Pearl shook out two pills and handed them to her sister. She picked up the water glass from the bedside table and held it while Winnie put the pills on her tongue. She sipped at the water.

Even swallowing was an effort.

Pearl waited until the pills went down, and Winnie was settled beneath clean sheets, before she closed the blinds and walked to the door.

"I'll be back in an hour," she said, but Winnie was already asleep.

Henry was sitting in the kitchen, waiting for her, two cups and a pot of cozied tea on the table in front of him, a pile of muddy vegetables dumped into the sink behind him. Pearl pointed a finger at them.

"Couldn't you have cleaned that mess up?" she said, her voice getting louder as she stomped over to the sink. "What the hell's wrong with you, Henry? And what the hell is wrong with that sister of yours? This place is a pigsty, and she sits around reading movie magazines. That girl up there can't do a thing for herself. Is she blind, your sister, or is she just stupid?"

Henry sighed. "It's no good yelling at me. Jolene's a strange one, but at least she's here."

"Oh, and I'm not. Is that what you're saying? Is that it?"

"No, Pearl, that's not what I'm saying." Henry lifted the cozy off the pot and poured himself a cup of tea. "Now come over here and sit down. Tell me what's really going on."

Pearl ignored him, stood at the sink and turned on the tap. She watched as bright, clear well water dissolved the mud from the vegetables and sluiced down the drain, the cloudy colour of spring runoff. Her mother had taken ill in the spring, and she might have lasted until winter had it not been for Pearl's father.

Pearl turned off the tap.

"I want to take her home. Darlene can sleep in our room, and Winnie can have her bed."

Henry shook his head. "I don't know, Pearl. How does Winnie feel about that? And what about Jolene? She's the one who's looking after her."

"Looking after her? For Christ's sake, Henry, look around. Winnie needs constant care now. And Jolene clearly can't do that."

"But this is her home. This is where she belongs. If it were me, I'd want to be dying in my own bed."

"Well, she's not you. She'll see the sense of it. I know she will."

Henry put his teacup down, got to his feet and placed his hands on her shoulders. "Do me a favour, Pearl. Don't go getting your hopes up. I'd hate to see you disappointed if she says no."

"Oh, she'll say yes. I know she will." Pearl took Henry's hands in her own and leaned forward to kiss his cheek. "Thank you, Henry," she said.

Henry nodded, and she left him standing there, staring at his teacup, the same worried look still pulling at his face.

They waited until five thirty. When Jolene still hadn't shown up, they sat down and had their dinner. Pearl had been in and out of Winnie's room every hour on the hour, but each time she checked in, Winnie had been sound asleep. Now, she stood at the bedroom window, listening to her sister's breathing, staring at the thunderclouds that were rolling in from the northwest. It looked as if someone had drawn a line through the heavens, a line like the demarcation between the future and the past: one half as black as earth, the other half the colour of a pale blue delphinium. And as the boiling mass of clouds overtook the sun, a sudden shaft of yellow light lit the fields and the trees below. The sky rumbled, coughed, and a puff of icy air blew in through the open window. Then the rain came, intermittently at first, in fat single drops that splattered against the veranda roof below. Then in a clatter of hailstones the size of marbles and moth balls that bounced across its shingles. Finally in a torrent that slammed into the earth and blotted out the horizon.

In her mind's eye, Pearl could see the once plump seed heads at the side of the road blasted by the hail, sagging to the ground under the weight of the rain, taking with them the hopes of the farmers who had planted them. Despite the relief of the cool rain's breeze, Pearl slammed the window shut and closed her eyes against the fierce splendour of the storm.

This was why she had left this godforsaken place: because despite its wild and wide-open beauty, its sudden cruelty was more than any human being should ever have to bear.

"Do you remember when we were kids? How we used to pray for rain?"

Pearl turned around and smiled at her sister. "You're awake," she said, pointing at the table next to the bed. "There's some soup there. If it's cold, I can warm it up again."

"Maybe later," Winnie said as she shifted her body, trying to find a comfortable position.

"Here. Let me help you with that."

"No, wait," Winnie said. "Please. Open the window again. I want to hear the rain."

"It'll drench the sill, Winnie. It'll get all over the floor,"

"I don't care about that," Winnie said and smiled at Pearl the way she had always smiled when she was a girl. "I just want to hear it."

Pearl yanked the window open again, and the room swirled with the sound of rushing water, the smell of damp earth and a cool breeze that pushed aside the stale, hot air of the sick room. Pearl leaned in and drew a deep, clean breath.

"The wind's changed direction," she said and turned to look at Winnie. Her sister's face had more colour now; her eyes were brighter, more alive. "I'll plump the pillows for you," Pearl said. "Take hold of my arm and sit up for a minute, and I'll freshen them for you."

Winnie wrapped both her arms around Pearl's and stared at the open window. "Remember how many times we did this for Mom?"

"No," Pearl said, shaking out the pillows with more force than was needed. "I don't remember. I think you were the one who did most of that."

"You were so young." Winnie sighed and sank back against her pillows. "My God. It must have been terrible for her, knowing she had to leave us all, and there was nothing she could do."

Pearl turned away from her sister and walked back to the open window. The rain had reduced to a patter now, and a soft white mist hugged the ground. Dark water dripped from the eaves, pooled in the potholes along the dirt road, swelled in the leaf-blocked gutters at the edge of the roof.

Winnie spoke to her back. "He must have loved her, don't you think, Pearl? He must have loved her to have done what he did."

Pearl wanted to plug her ears and yell at her sister to shut up and stop telling such awful lies. Instead, she wrapped her arms around her stomach to protect her unborn child from the terrible feelings that were gathering and spreading through her mother's body like a storm. But it did no good. The baby started kicking again, pumping her legs like a frantic swimmer, pummelling at the side of Pearl's stomach with a small fisted hand. Pearl took a deep breath and tried to keep her body still as she turned to face her sister.

"He was a nasty, self-centred son of a bitch. And nothing you say will ever convince me otherwise. Who knows how long she might have lived if it hadn't been for him?"

"But she was dying, Pearl."

"And he was too gutless to let her die in peace. Too much of a coward to stick around and look after his own kids."

Winnie stared at her hands and shook her head. "Poor Pearl." She closed her eyes, leaned her head against her pillows and patted the bed. "Come and talk to me. Tell me everything. Tell me everything I've missed."

Pearl turned back to the window. Everything outside was glistening now, dripping with water, the grass, the trees, even the shingles on the veranda roof. Everything looked shiny and new.

"What's to tell? You left and I got by. The war ended and I married Henry. That's pretty much it."

"Do you remember when we were kids? How we used to say that we'd live in houses side by side? Yours would be white with blue trim and mine would be white with red."

Pearl stared at the new world and the dying sun and turned to face her sister. "I want you to come and live with us, Winnie. The doctors in the city are better than the quacks out here. Maybe there's a new treatment you could try. And if you live with us, you could get to know Darlene. I can look after you. I want to look after you."

Winnie sighed. "I can't do that, Pearl," she said.

"Why not? It's crazy, you staying here. We're your family. You should be with us."

Winnie closed her eyes. "Jolene's my family too."

"Don't be ridiculous. Jolene's not your goddamned family. She's a friend and a bloody useless one, if you ask me. She can't care for you properly. Not like I can."

"But she needs me, Pearl. And I love her. I love her the way Henry loves you."

"Oh, for Christ's sake, stop talking such nonsense. You don't love Jolene like that. You can't. You're just making this up because you're angry with me. You're angry because I never answered any of your goddamned letters. Well, I'm not the one who left you, Winnie. You left me. And mark my words. As soon as Jolene finds a man, she'll be up and gone too. And who's going to look after you then?"

Winnie's face was grey now, as grey as the rain clouds that had come and gone. "No, Pearl. She won't leave me. She may not love me the way I love her, but she won't leave. She'd never do that."

Pearl watched as Winnie closed her eyes and laid her head on the pillows, the skin of her face sagging away from the bone, exposing the lines of her skull. Pearl ran to the bureau and grabbed the pill container, but her hands were shaking so badly that she lost her grip. The pills burst out of the bottle and scattered to the ground. Sliding her hand down the side of the bureau, she lowered her pregnant body and got onto her hands and knees to gather them up, her tears spattering like rain across the linoleum floor. She got up, wiped them away and took two pills to her sister.

"Take these," she said, stroking Winnie's head. "Take them and get some rest."

Pearl woke up at midnight where she'd fallen asleep in the chair next to Winnie's bed. Her neck was aching, and her back felt as if someone had shoved hot coals along the base of her spine. It wasn't until she stood up and stretched that she heard the sound of the truck rattling along the dirt road. She walked into the pool of moonlight next to the open window just as the truck slid across the loose gravel and came to a lurching stop. Jolene's window was down, the radio was on, and Kitty Wells was belting out a song into the still prairie night. Pearl waited until the music stopped and the door swung open, Jolene swinging out with it. She staggered, grabbed hold of the door-frame to steady herself then slammed it shut. Pumping her purse up and down at her side, she sang as she wove her way up the path toward the house.

"It wasn't God who made honky-tonk angels, as you sing in the words of your song…"

Pearl walked into the upstairs hallway and listened. The front door opened, clicked shut, and she could hear Jolene humming as she started up the stairs. There were three bedrooms on the second floor, Jolene's, Winnie's and the one where Henry now slept. She could hear him snoring as she backed into the room and stood in the darkness, watching as Jolene staggered up the last stair and onto the landing. Jolene stopped, feet locked to the floor, body circling in the air like the last slow turns of a spinning top. She stared through the open doorway that led to Winnie's room then disappeared inside. Pearl could hear her kick off her shoes, the sound of fabric falling to the floor, the wheezing wire sound of bedsprings, then silence.

Pearl stood alone in the darkness, as alone as she'd ever felt in her life. Then she stepped out of her shoes, walked across the hallway and looked into her sister's room. She could see two bodies lit by moonlight, Winnie floating on her back, hands at her sides, Jolene lying on her stomach like a drowned woman, one hand hanging over the edge of the bed, the other holding fast to Winnie's arm.

Pearl turned around and walked back to her own room. She got up onto the bed and squeezed Henry's shoulder. He woke up with a start and turned toward her.

"What? What's wrong? Are you all right?"

"I want to go home, Henry," she said. "I want to go home."

Henry sat up, wrapped his arms around her and held her while she wept.

The next morning, Henry had the trunk open and was loading the car when Jolene appeared in the doorway of the house, carrying a cardboard box. She staggered a little, either under its weight or the lingering effects of the alcohol she'd consumed the night before. When she got to the spot where Pearl was standing, she thrust the box at her.

"She wants you to have this," she said.

"What for?" Pearl asked. "I told her this morning. I'll be back in a couple of weeks. I can get it then."

Jolene just shook her head as if she knew things Pearl was too foolish to understand or too stubborn to see. "I think you'd better take it now," she said, placing the box at Pearl's feet. She turned away, took a few steps then glanced over her shoulder. "You could have brought the child, you know. I wouldn't have tried to take her back."

Before Pearl could respond, Jolene raised an arm at Henry and shouted, "See you later, brother."

"I'll be back out when I can, Jolene," Henry called back. He slammed the trunk shut and walked over to Pearl. "What's in that?" he asked, pointing at the box.

Pearl bent over as best she could, opened the flaps and stared at the contents of the box: a book, a pocket watch, a packet of letters, silver shears, and a pink and blue rag rug.

Pearl straightened her back and looked at Henry. "Just put it in the goddamned trunk," she said and started toward the car. "And when we get home, throw it out. I never want to see it again."

CHAPTER 14

2000

She was submerged, dreaming that her body was floating
in lukewarm water, when the ringing started: soft at first,
then louder, like an angry wasp boring into her auditory
nerve. She opened her eyes and listened. Was it ringing or
groaning or both?

"For Christ's sake, Carol. Aren't you going to answer
that?"

She could feel the bed beneath her now, heard the bur-
ring drone of the phone. She reached for the receiver, mum-
bled hello, then sat up straight to listen, wondering if she
might still be dreaming, if the too-calm voice at the other
end of the line was real or another auditory hallucination.

"Did you hear me, Mrs. Bukowski? Can you come now?"

Carol opened her mouth and felt the air, heavy as water,
rush into her lungs. "Yes. Yes, I'll be there as fast as I can."

As she hung up the phone, Nathan groaned. "Who the
hell was that?"

"The hospital," she said, heaving her legs out of bed. "It's my mother. Something's wrong."

There was another groan. "Oh, Christ. Why now? Why tonight?"

"Go back to sleep, Nathan," Carol said as she groped her way through the watery darkness. "No one asked you to come."

She reached the closet and flicked on the light, wincing against its dry, harsh glare. Once her eyes adjusted, she went through the motions of choosing her clothes: a pair of pants, a shirt and sandals. She could hear Nathan talking in the next room, something about a meeting in the morning and a quarterly report, but she couldn't quite register what he was saying. The air pressed against her eardrums, and everything she looked at seemed distant and distorted as if she were staring through a fisheye lens. No matter how fast she tried to pull on her pants, fasten her shirt and slip on her shoes, her fingers refused to bend, her limbs resisted movement. She tore off the blouse she was trying to button and pulled on a T-shirt instead.

She was crossing the room when Nathan sat up in bed. "Well? Do you want me to come or not?"

"No," Carol said and closed the bedroom door behind her.

By the time she got to the kitchen, she was fully alert and trembling. She grabbed the phone and dialed Darlene's home number. No answer. She hung up and misdialed her sister's cell phone number three times before she finally got it right. It rang twice.

"Answer it, Darlene. Answer it."

It rang one more time, and a voice cut in. "The cellular

customer you have reached has the phone turned off. Please try again."

Carol stared at the phone, then raised it above her head and slammed it into the smooth granite surface of the kitchen counter over and over again, until the incessant electronic bleating finally brought her to her senses. She dropped the phone onto the counter and stepped back, horrified. Reaching out, she pressed what was left of the off button and stood there staring into the dark and empty room. The refrigerator hummed, and the blue numbers on the stove clock glowed like a beacon. Twenty minutes since the hospital had called, and she was still standing in the kitchen.

She grabbed her purse, took out her cell phone and dialed her sister's home number again, waiting this time until the message cut in. "It's Carol," she said as she hurried out the kitchen door into the garage. "I need you, Darlene. I need you to come to the hospital."

Carol swung her car out of the driveway and onto the street. Every house on the crescent was dark and silent. She thought about the people inside those houses, eyes closed, sleeping peacefully. Hers was a good street, a safe street, one where mothers drove their kids to school in minivans, and fathers kept the lawns mowed, the trim painted and the gardens neatly edged. Everything was in order, everything in good repair. Chaos was something that lived over there, far beyond the boundaries of the Maple Ridge suburb. It lived in distant neighbourhoods like the one where Carol had grown up.

"How can you stand living in a place like this?" her sister asked the day she moved in. "It has no character."

Carol watched the houses slide by her car window and

tried to see what Darlene had seen. She had been delighted when she and Nathan purchased their second home. It was newer and grander than anything she had ever imagined herself living in.

"You'll never stop cleaning it," her mother had said. "It's too goddamned big."

Carol flicked on her turn signal and took a right onto The Boulevard. There was no pleasing her family, no way to impress them either, and she found herself wondering why she had ever bothered to try.

Irritated by the cold blast of the air conditioning, she hit the off button, opened the window and checked her rear-view mirror. There were only a couple of cars on the street and no sign of the police, so she pressed her foot down on the accelerator. The night wind blew across her face and shoulders, as fresh and crisp as rain-cleansed air. She held her arm out the window and opened her hand, feeling the slipstream push against her fingers, bend around her cupped palm. The easy, gliding motion of the car and the tangible weight of the air calmed her, and she slowed to the speed limit.

No sense getting a ticket. Her mother would no doubt survive.

Ten minutes later, she approached the city centre. She rolled her window back up and locked her doors. The hospital was located close to her mother's neighbourhood, an area of town that had once been filled with working people and immigrants and was now populated by biker gangs and terrified welfare moms.

"Why do you stay here, Mother?" she'd asked. "Why don't you move into a nice little apartment near us?"

"Because I like it here," Pearl said. "And I won't be pushed out by some hoodlum on a motorbike."

She knew that her mother had been referring to Carol's first husband, Phillip. Phillip had always driven a Harley.

Carol gripped the steering wheel and thought about the newspaper clipping she'd hidden at the bottom of her lingerie drawer a few days earlier. It was a wedding notice, the one she had been waiting to read for almost twenty-five years. The day she found it she had opened the newspaper and on impulse turned to the obituaries. She had scanned the names and photos of the deceased, then skipped over to the engagement and wedding announcements on the opposite page, wondering, as she often did, why they put all those happy, smiling faces of girls in bridal veils right next to all those dead people. Then she spotted Phillip's middle-aged face among the smiling future grooms and understood.

Perhaps there was always someone for whom a wedding notice signalled a kind of death.

She had cut the announcement out of the paper, stuffed it into the bottom of her drawer and cried, off and on, for the rest of the day.

By the time she pulled into the hospital parking lot, Carol's palms were damp and her heart was racing again. She drove her car into an empty space near the entrance, got out and hurried through the doors to the elevators. She pressed the button, pressed it again and waited, watching the descending numbers light up as the carriage dropped from the fourth to the third, the second to the first.

Hurry up. Hurry the hell up.

The bell dinged, the doors opened, and Carol was forced to wait as an elderly man got off the elevator escorted by a middle-aged woman. Both of them were crying. Carol

watched as they crossed the foyer and wondered who
had died.

She got into the elevator, pressed five and thought
about her father's death. She had visited him only once
the week he died, because she couldn't face his pain or
the terrible transformation his body had undergone. But
her father had waited for her, waited until she was there
to hold his hand, touch his face and watch him die. He'd
rallied once that night and opened his eyes.

"Tell the English lady to take the flowers from my
mouth," he'd whispered to her, and twenty minutes later
he was dead.

Where had he been? she wondered. Was it a ritual he
had seen as a child, like the placing of coins on the eyes of
the dead? Or was he simply unable to breathe? Or was his
last request an apprehension of what was to come: a body
buried in soil, a mouth filled with earth and root?

Carol gripped the metal railing as the elevator bounced
to a stop. The doors opened, and she peered into the hallway. The nursing station was empty, the ward lights dim,
the air beyond the elevator heavy with the odour of sickness
and death. She stepped out and looked down the hallway.
A crash cart was sitting outside her mother's room, and
two nurses were standing beside it. Her mother's physician,
Dr. Weinman, stepped out of the room, said something to
the nurses, and they followed him back inside.

"You're not related to Harry Weinman, are you?" her
mother had asked when she awoke to find herself in the
hospital. "The one who owned Mrs. Day's?"

Carol had cringed.

Mrs. Day's was the discount clothing store where her
mother had taken Carol and Darlene every second year to
buy their new winter coats. It was the only extravagant

thing her mother had ever done, buying them each new coats rather than forcing her to wear her sister's hand-me-downs as she did with almost every other article of clothing Carol wore, save her underwear.

"A winter coat's different," her mother would say. "That's the first thing people see."

So every second year, for the first twelve years of her life, Carol had looked forward to the trip to Mrs. Day's with a kind of choked anticipation. Cramped and jam-packed with endless racks of dresses and skirts, coats and jackets of every cut and style, Mrs. Day's always smelt of damp wooden floors, fusty wool and tetrachloride. But as a child, Carol had loved it. She loved roaming the aisles, eyes feeding on myriad colours, small fingers reaching out to feel the fabrics, knobby as carpet, slippery as hair, equally dazzled by the words that rolled from Mr. Weinman's tongue like the names of exotic birds: peau de soie, crepe de chine, tweed. Once, he described a coat as camel's hair, and she had reached out to touch it, imagining herself a desert princess in the oasis she had drawn for her grade three geography project, "Places of the World."

But the year she turned thirteen, everything had changed. Driving to Mrs. Day's with her mother at the wheel of their 1949 Chevy Deluxe, she had stared out the window at the dilapidated buildings of the warehouse district, wanting to dissolve into the grey, pinstriped fabric of the passenger seat. This was where the poor people shopped: not at Clifford's Lady's Wear, not at the downtown Hudson's Bay store, but in the sweatshop outlets of the city's north and west end.

"Oh, for goodness' sakes, Mother, there are hundreds of people named Weinman," she had said with a derisive laugh, hoping to stave off any embarrassment the cardiologist might feel at being associated with the proprietor of Mrs. Day's. "It doesn't mean they're all related."

To Carol's surprise, the cardiologist smiled. "That was my dad. Did you know him, Mrs. Calder?"

"Know him? Damned right, I knew him. Bought more winter coats from that man than I can count. Always got a discount, though. Loved to haggle, that father of yours." Pearl wagged an index finger at him. "But he was good to his customers. Yes, he was a good man, your father." She looked up at him, pressed her lips together and made a loud clacking sound at the corner of her mouth. "And now his son is a doctor. He must have been proud of that."

"Not a Jewish father on the planet who wouldn't be, Mrs. Calder," Dr. Weinman said with a laugh.

Her mother had laughed along with him, then thrust a thumb at Carol. "Now if I'd said that, she'd have been trying to shut me up. But like I've always said, there's nobody funnier than a Jew. All my favourite comedians are Jewish. Always have been."

Carol stood there, wanting the floor to crack open and swallow her whole, until she realized that Dr. Weinman was still laughing.

"You've got that right. Now let's open up that gown of yours so I can get a good look," he said, waggling the end of his stethoscope at her. "I mean a good listen."

From that point on, Dr. Weinman had dropped by her mother's room whenever he got the chance. Even the nurses had commented on it: "I can page that man fifty times for another patient, but if I page him for your mother, he's here in fifteen seconds flat."

Carol started to run down the hallway toward her mother's room, hoping to God that Dr. Weinman had responded as quickly tonight. When she raced through the door, he looked up, waved her in, and the nurses turned to leave.

Carol could barely breathe. "Is she all right?" she asked.

Dr. Weinman shook his head.

Carol moved toward her mother. The lights were low and the covers on the bed had been tucked in tight around Pearl's body. Motionless hands lay on top of folded sheets. An oxygen mask hid her nose and mouth, its green-tinged plastic turning the pale skin of Pearl's cheeks the colour of an unripe pear.

"It was a heart attack this time," Dr. Weinman said. "I'm afraid it's not good."

"Will she wake up?" Carol asked.

"We're waiting for a bed in ICU," he said, avoiding her gaze. "You might want to notify the rest of your family."

"There's just my sister. I called, but I couldn't reach her, so I left a message."

"I'll tell the nurses. They'll send her in as soon as she arrives."

Carol stared at his weary face. "Are you all right?"

Dr. Weinman smiled and shrugged his shoulders. "Some patients just matter more than others," he said. "I'll let you know when we're ready to move her."

Carol watched him walk away, his gait stiff with failure and regret. She wondered why her mother mattered so much to this man. What had he seen that she had always failed to see? She looked down at the woman in the bed. It had been so long since she had touched her mother, but she needed to touch her now, so she reached out to stroke her brow and her thin, brittle hair.

"It's Carol, Mom," she whispered.

She took her mother's hand and watched as Pearl's fingers slowly folded inward to embrace her own.

CHAPTER 15

1939

She loved the feel of the treadle beneath her feet, the perfect roll and pitch of its belted weight pushing against the
heel then toe of her shoe. She loved the sound the machine
made as the wheel turned and the needle rose and fell in
time to her rocking feet, marking its perfect stitches down
the length of braided cloth. That whirring, thumping
sound blocked out so many others: the snap of the screen
door, the rhythmic pounding of her husband's footsteps,
the voices of her children.

Every morning, Lettie prepared the machine for work:
filling the bobbins, threading the needle, adjusting the
tension and drive belt. Once a month, she would flush the
oil ports with kerosene and clean every moving part down
to the metal. On those days, she ran the machine for a
few minutes just as the manual instructed then wiped it
down and waited, oiling it later, when the gas had evap-
orated and the metal was dry. Then she would lubricate

the machine every other day, especially on days when she felt well enough to sew.

Those days were becoming less and less frequent now. Most mornings she had only enough strength to make a pot of poppy tea and sleep the day away, rising only when the kids returned home from school.

Today hadn't been too bad.

She turned to look at the clock on her bedside table. It was one p.m. Lots of time before the girls came home from school, banging through the door, rattling through the cupboards and the ice box, looking for something to tide them over until dinner.

Lettie swung her legs over the side of the bed, shuffled into the kitchen and lifted the trap door that led to the root cellar. She would bake a few pies, using up the preserves from last year to make way for the crabapple jelly that was bubbling on the stove. She and Winnie had put the dills up a few weeks before, when the cucumbers were crisp and fresh, and she had made a few pots of jam: strawberry in July, raspberry and blueberry at the height of the season, when she'd been well enough to pick them. In the coming weeks, she would can the last of the beans and make her sweet pickles and tomato and onion relish. In a week or two, she would ask Matthew to dig up the last of the root vegetables and haul them down into the furthest corner of the cellar, where they would keep well into the winter.

Lettie turned her back to the trap door, eased herself into a crouch and tented her fingers on the floor, feeling for the first ladder rung with her toe. Once it lodged against her heel, she began the climb down, one cautious step at a time. When both feet were safely on the dirt floor, she stood in the darkness and listened. A small scratching sound resonated from the far corner of the cellar, a mouse, perhaps, or a vole. She would have to send William down with more traps and enough steel wool to plug the holes or they would lose this year's vegetables. She moved, something snapped and the scrabbling sound stopped. Lettie took a deep breath, her nose filling with the sharp scent of damp soil and decaying wood, and it seemed as if the cellar walls were moving toward her. That the ceiling, like a heavy lid, was closing shut above her head. Her arms flew up from her sides, hands searching the air for the sharp edge of the shelf where she kept the matches. Her fingers touched wood and fumbled across its surface, feeling along the length of the shelf until her fingertips tapped against a small box. Hands shaking, she slid the cardboard pocket open, pulled out a match, and hit it hard against the striker. The cellar snapped back into focus, the walls returning to a safe distance, the ceiling opening up to a comfortable height above her head.

Lettie leaned against the shelf to steady herself. Dying would come soon enough, and fear might hasten its coming. Better to think about living, to revel in its evidence arrayed in the glass jars that lined the shelves above her head: the whole, sweetened crabapples she'd put up last year, the dandelion wine and raspberry cordial she kept for special occasions, and next to them, a quart sealer jar of blueberry preserves left over from last season.

Blueberry pie was Pearl's favourite, so Lettie would make that, maybe stretch it to two pies if she made a thick enough glaze with the liquid. She took the jar and turned back to the narrow stepladder. How many times had she climbed its rungs with no effort at all? Now, just the thought exhausted her.

Grabbing hold of the middle rung with her free hand,

she started up. There was no point wasting time on self-pity. She had pies to bake, a dinner to cook, jars to sterilize and three children and a husband to feed. There would be plenty of time for worrying when she lay in bed at night, unable to sleep.

It was Pearl who worried her most. Just that morning she'd heard her daughters arguing.

"You have to go in," Winnie said.

"Why should I? She doesn't get up to see me. She doesn't even cook our breakfast any more."

"Go in and say goodbye, Pearl."

"Bye, Mom!" Pearl shouted, and the screen door slammed shut behind her.

Winnie popped her head in the bedroom door. "She's got a spelling test and has to get in early. Is there anything you need?"

"Just this," Lettie said, wrapping her arms around Winnie's sturdy frame and whispering into her ear. "Don't be too hard on her. She's just a little girl. She doesn't understand."

Winnie stood back and stared at her hands. "Maybe you should tell her."

"Tell her what?"

"That you're sick. That you might not get well."

Lettie smiled and cupped her fingers under her daughter's chin. "Don't be silly. I'll get well. It's just a matter of time. Now off you go. I'll see you when you get home."

Winnie's face hadn't brightened as it usually did. Instead, she stared at Lettie as if to say, *Why do you lie to me?*

Lifting a jar out of the sterilizing bath, Lettie rested a clean metal funnel in its throat and began ladling in the boiling jelly. She hadn't told the children, and she had made William promise not to tell them either. So how could Winnie know? Unless William's crepe-hanging mother had told them. She put the ladle down and leaned against the side of the counter. It would be just like William's mother to do something like that. Gather the children together and tell them that their papist mother was preparing to go to hell.

Lettie reached into her pocket and fingered her rosary. How would the children manage without her? How would William cope with them, when he could barely cope with himself? She had wanted to write to her own family and ask if they would take the children, but William wouldn't hear of it. He kept insisting that they were his kids and his responsibility. But the children had always been hers: hers to rear and protect, hers to keep safe. And even in this she had failed. She had failed to protect her son, and now, in dying, she would fail to protect Pearl.

Sometimes it seemed to Lettie that Pearl had been born afraid. How she had clung to Lettie, hiding behind her legs when people came to visit, never allowing her mother too far from her sight. Pearl had cried so hard on the first day of school that Lettie thought her own heart would break, but in the end, she had walked away from her youngest daughter and left her there. That night, when Pearl arrived home, and Lettie knelt down to ask about her day, her youngest daughter had crossed her arms and looked away. So Lettie got to her feet and walked toward the kitchen, and Pearl had raced across the room, flinging herself against her mother's legs.

Lettie had laughed as she bent down to gather her daughter into her arms, and Pearl nestled her nose into Lettie's neck.

"Don't make me go back," she whispered.

Lettie looked at her two older children and pointed at the door. "Play outside, you two."

When they were gone, Lettie carried Pearl to the rocker in the living room and sat down. "You have to go to school, Pearl."

"But why? Why can't I stay with you?"

"Because you have to learn to read and write so you won't be like me. I never learned to read and write, and I'm sad about that every single day."

Pearl clapped her hands together. "Then you can come with me. You can learn too."

Lettie smiled at her daughter. "I'm too old for that. So you'll have to go and learn for me."

Pearl stared at her hands. "I don't think so."

Lettie could hear the potato pot boiling over on the stove, so she lifted Pearl from her lap and set her on the floor. "No more arguments," she said.

"No!" Pearl shouted, flinging herself on the floor. "I won't go. I'm staying here with you!"

"You're going, Pearl, and that's an end to it." Lettie turned and walked away, leaving her daughter where she lay on the floor in a sobbing heap.

Half an hour later, when dinner was ready, she went back into the living room to find Pearl lying where she had left her, thumb in her mouth, fast asleep. Lettie tried to wake her, but Pearl just rubbed her eyes.

"You don't love me," she said.

From that day on, Pearl had been a different girl: tougher, sassier, no longer her mother's baby. But Lettie knew that the shy and fearful child still lived at the heart of Pearl, and as her illness worsened, her daughter's fear had grown into a fierce and petulant rage. Now she barely looked at Lettie, and she rarely spoke to her.

And perhaps that was for the best. Anger was like armour. Not the best protection, but a shield nonetheless.

Lettie poured hot wax across the cooling surface of the jelly, placed a rubber ring on the neck of the jar and screwed down the glass lid. In this and other ways, Pearl was like her father. Lettie had sensed it the first time she met William, sensed that his closed expression and the angry set of his mouth belied a sorrow that hid at the back of his eyes like a small and frightened animal. Had she known the real depth of William's anger, she might never have married him. Instead, she had fixed her eyes on that small, timid thing, trying to coax it out, hoping it would emerge from its burrow and bring with it the true and gentle soul of her husband. Instead, the small thing had wasted away and died of fear.

The war had done that to William. It had taken most of who he was. Then the drought and the dust took the rest. He never spoke of the war, never told her what he had survived, but she knew because she felt it in the thrashing of his limbs and the cries of the men who woke him in the darkest hours of the night.

She turned the lids tight then a quarter back until the jars cooled. She glanced out the kitchen window at the yard. There was no sign of William or her son. She would have to get the vegetables herself, so she took the colander down from the hook where it hung, made her way down the front hall and out the door. Leaning against the porch post, she scanned the yard and the fields beyond. No sign of them.

Lettie stared down the length of the porch to the tall, straight rows of corn at the end of her vegetable garden. Perhaps it wasn't that far. Perhaps she would make it. She began to walk, but by the time she reached the porch stairs, she desperately needed to rest. She looked around for the wicker chair that usually sat nearby, but someone had moved it. Probably one of the kids. So she gripped the stair post, eased her thin and tired body down onto the top step and looked out over her garden.

· This season, everything was high and heavy – heavy with seedpods and fruit, exuberance and abundance. How could a seed as small as a speck of dirt produce such height and profusion? Corn kernels, no bigger than the tip of her baby finger, that had shot up to a six-foot height of green. It was a miracle, really. *An incredible miracle and a comfort as well*, she thought as she rose to her feet to move down the stairs, into the garden and deep into the rows of corn. The edges of the husks and the sharp spears of the leaves were just beginning to turn colour: their deep green pigments fading to a brittle brown at the tip. And as she walked amid the corn, the ripening tangle of pumpkin and squash, the vines heavy with pods of yellow and green, the garden told her its story: a story of joy and solace and grief. And finally, when she could walk and stand no longer, when the full force of the pain broke through the barrier of the medicine she had taken, Lettie sat down on the sun-warmed earth, the earth from which she came and to which she would soon return, and thought to herself that it really didn't matter if she ever stood again.

It was then she heard the footsteps, solid and heavy, sounding down the length of the porch. An old woman was walking toward her, backlit by the sun. The woman stopped at the top of the stairs, raised a fleshy arm as if to wave and called out to her, "Get up, Mom! I'll be home soon."

Who is she? Lettie wondered. The thought no sooner entered her head than the woman was gone, and all she could hear was the sound of running feet, followed by the flash of a white blouse, the kicking pleats of a navy blue tunic. A pair of scuffed brown shoes appeared at her knee.

"What are you doing?" a soft and frightened voice asked. "Why are you sitting on the ground?"

Lettie shielded her eyes, looked up at Pearl and smiled. "I was waiting for you," she said.

ACKNOWLEDGEMENTS

Heartfelt thanks to the members of my Halifax writing group – Renee Hartleib, Janice Acton, Michelle Mulder and Binnie Brennan – for their invaluable insight, support and friendship throughout the writing of this book. Thanks also to Carol Bruneau and Sandra McIntyre who attended Pearl's birth, and to my new friends and colleagues, Anne Lazurko, Nina Levitt and all of the other, talented writers at Sage Hill, who were there for the birth of the final chapter. The Manitoba and Winnipeg Arts Councils offered me financial assistance to attend the Sage Hill Experience workshops, and for that I am very grateful.

I owe a huge debt of gratitude to the many authors I love, and who have inspired me. Among them, my kind, astute and meticulous editor, Helen Humphreys, who identified the critical missing scenes, and my talented sister, Margaret, who led the way.

To all of my family and friends in Montreal, Winnipeg and beyond: thank you so much for being there and for cheering me on. To my life partner and best friend, Brian: no amount of thanks could ever fully convey my gratitude. You are, in every sense, the heart of my home.

Finally, while the city featured in this book is Winnipeg, the street names and neighbourhoods are fictional. You will not find them on any map, save the one in your imagination.

ABOUT THE AUTHOR

Let Us Be True is Erna Buffie's first novel. Over the past 25 years, she has written, directed and produced numerous award-winning documentary films for broadcasters around the world, and has interviewed some of the world's most interesting scientists and thinkers, including Gloria Steinam and Jane Goodall. In 2013, she won the award for Best Direction in a Documentary at the 2013 Canadian Screen Awards for her film *Smarty Plants.*

Erna lived in Montreal for 20 years, and in a seaside home just outside of Halifax, for seven. In 2011, she decided to return to the prairies and the city where she was born and raised. She now divides her time between Winnipeg and a small cottage on Long Pine Lake in the Whiteshell, which she shares with her husband and their little grey mutt.

FSC

www.fsc.org

MIX

Paper from
responsible sources

FSC® C016245

ENVIRONMENTAL BENEFITS STATEMENT

Coteau Books saved the following resources by printing the pages of this book on chlorine free paper made with 100% post-consumer waste.

TREES	WATER	ENERGY	SOLID WASTE	GREENHOUSE GASES
6	2,883	2	193	532
FULLY GROWN	GALLONS	MILLION BTUs	POUNDS	POUNDS

 Environmental impact estimates were made using the Environmental Paper Network Paper Calculator 3.2. For more information visit www.papercalculator.org.